CW00858315

BUTTERFLIES BLUE

CHAMBERS LANE SERIES BOOK 4

DANIEL MALDONADO

This book is dedicated to a special woman who taught me patience, forgiveness, the value of listening and being a friend, even when longings and desires were present and needed to be subdued. May you have the rebirth and love of life that you deserve.

CONTENT ADVISORY

This book is intended for mature audiences and contains graphic violence, explicit language, and disturbing imagery.

OLD SAN JUAN

OLD SAN JUAN, PUERTO RICO

Present Day

THE BLUE AND purplish cobblestones that laced the long, hilly street called *Calle del Cristo* by the original Spanish inhabitants glistened brightly as Layla gently strolled along the road. She was arm in arm with her new man, Daniel. Daniel was a burly, bronzed Hispanic male whose light brown eyes occasionally gazed deeply towards her as they walked. They had only been walking the streets of Old San Juan that afternoon for a few minutes when Layla heard the bustling noise of locals eagerly setting up tents for an event.

"Look. It must be starting soon," Layla said as she smiled and gently squeezed Daniel's arm. He was not startled but sensed her excitement.

"Yes, dear. Looks like they'll be ready in a few hours."

Daniel pointed to the red and blue banner flapping in the brisk easterly Caribbean winds. The winds not only brought the new couple coolness and relief from the warm November day but also a saltiness that they could smell and even taste in the air. The banner revealed that the San Juan annual culinary arts festival would begin at five p.m. and last well into the night.

"Do you want to go? We can eat some local cuisine," Daniel asked, awaiting her response.

"Hmm, that would be interesting. I've never had Puerto Rican food. How is it?"

"I think you'll love it."

Even though he had never lived on the island, Daniel had traveled to Puerto Rico on several occasions and enjoyed eating his people's traditional food. He also enjoyed cooking Puerto Rican food and sharing that experience with his friends and family.

"There is a dish that you should try. *Mofongo.* It's made with plantains, which are green bananas, and topped with whatever meats you want."

"Can they top it with fish?" Layla inquired.

Daniel was amused and smiled. He knew that Layla recently started only eating fish. She was a pescatarian, but he secretly wanted her to try different foods on this trip. "Sure. You can get *mofongo* with fish. But you can also have it topped with other seafood: crab, lobster, conch, shrimp... or even pork or chicken. You can get any flavor that the Caribbean offers."

Despite her reluctance on previous occasions to try new things when the couple dined out, Layla was now eager to step out of her comfort zone. She had only officially started seeing Daniel two months ago, although they had known each other for years. This was the first vacation that they planned together. She had always wanted to see places outside of the United States, especially exotic places that her friends had never traveled to before.

Once, Layla went on a day trip to Montreal when she first moved to New York about twenty years ago. But she did not consider that brief excursion to Canada anything extraordinary. There was something about Daniel's sense of excitement about his past travels around the world that challenged Layla and encouraged her to get away from it all. She wanted to get away from her work, the freezing, snowy winter, her family, and even the fears of past relationships. When Daniel offered to take her to Puerto Rico for Thanksgiving, she eagerly accepted.

"I think I'll try the conch. I don't even know what that is, but it's not anything that I've ever eaten before. It just has a sexy vibe to it." She giggled. She wanted to say that the word conch reminded her of the word for the male sexual organ, but her shyness and unfamiliarity with Daniel made her reluctant. Instead, she slyly asked, "Does it taste like gooey duck?"

Daniel visualized the large phallic mollusk with its lightly golden siphon and laughed. "No, honey. To be honest, I haven't eaten gooey duck before. I've seen it on TV with that bald-headed guy who eats all these strange foods. What's his name? I can't remember. He seemed to like it. I've always wanted to try it though."

Layla secretly loved that Daniel ate exotic foods from around the world, but she would never let him know. Years ago, he offered to cook her kangaroo *rendang*, a curry dish. Daniel found an Australian recipe on the internet adapting the traditional Indonesia one. He cooked it the previous year for himself and wanted to try it again. Daniel had explained to Layla how the lemongrass, coriander, and cumin seeds in the curry paste combined with the desiccated coconut flakes, coconut milk, and cardamom to give the kangaroo meat a fragrant taste. He loved it and thought that she would too. Layla, however, was reluctant to try anything so unfamiliar, especially because it was a friendly marsupial that Daniel recommended to consume. She derided that suggestion when he made it. But she was willing to eat conch for dinner later that night.

Because the festival was hours away, in the meantime, the two continued walking down *Calle del Cristo*. They could see signs for the various restaurants, art galleries, and boutiques that lined both sides of the street. Other travelers, who had disembarked from the cruise ship docked at the port of Old San Juan, were carrying shopping bags with purchases from the local craft and artisan shops. Layla decided that she wanted to look inside one shop to see what they had to offer. An electronic bell rang as she opened the door.

"Bueno. Welcome to our store." A skinny, pale Puerto Rican woman greeted them as they entered. She stood behind the cash register in the middle of the store checking out another patron. Both Layla and Daniel smiled at her and returned the greeting.

After looking around the small shop, Layla walked to the glass-encased jewelry display case near the front of the store. She looked haphazardly at the various items for sale, hoping to find something that she liked. Daniel dutifully followed her.

"You should get these," Daniel said as he pointed to a pair of oval-shaped earrings featuring a Puerto Rican flag. A white lone star was nearly centered in the triangular blue background. Three red stripes and two white stripes alternated to fill the remaining glossy background whose edges were scalloped.

Because they looked unique and were representative of their trip, Layla asked to try them on. Ultimately, she decided not to purchase them.

She then perused the far left corner of the store. There she saw numerous hand-carvings of the three wise men. Some carvings had a Puerto Rican flag situated in the middle of the base.

"Daniel, what are these?" Layla was unfamiliar with the story of Three Kings Day. So, Daniel proceeded to tell her of the celebration of the visit of the three magi when Jesus was born. He also explained that the holiday is traditionally celebrated on January 6 and that typically Puerto Rican's exchange gifts on Three Kings Day rather than on Christmas.

"We never celebrated it in my house. In fact, I never heard of it until I was an adult," Daniel added.

The two continued perusing the store, bought a few trinkets for themselves, and a gift for Layla's youngest daughter, Amirah. After completing their purchase, they walked further down *Calle del Cristo* past *Calle Fortaleza* until they reached the Chapel of Christ the Savior.

GRADUATION PARTY

GILBERT, ARIZONA

Three Years Earlier

"CAN we have the caterer set up the cake on the back table? I also want the bottle of Cristal placed in a champagne bucket near the head table. It's for Leon. The other champagne is for the guests. But this is my man's day and he deserves the best." Layla Little barked orders with determination. She had been planning this event for months ever since her long-term boyfriend, Leon Blackman, told her that he was finally graduating with his doctorate.

Never-mind that Leon didn't offer to pay for his own graduation party. Neither did his parents or the rest of his family. He seemed content to have Layla pay the full expense of his graduation party even though they were not officially a couple according to him. They had dated for two years now. Layla tried desperately to push any negative thoughts about Leon or his family's attitude from her mind. She would deal with them later once all of the hectic planning and celebrations were over. She focused only on the fact that her man was finally graduating and what that would mean for the future of their relationship. At least she hoped that the future was bright for both of them.

To show her commitment to the relationship, Layla took a temporary job in Arizona to be closer to Leon. The long-distance relationship was stressful and strained at times. Her grave-yard shift work schedule made it even more cumbersome. She slept during the days when Leon was working. And he slept when she was awake. Fortunately, her job in New York had a lateral position with a sister hospital in Tempe. Layla jumped at the opportunity to be closer to Leon. At first, he was reluctant and did not want her to take the job. Layla suspected that Leon was concerned about his reputation in the community. He did not want his congregation to see him with another woman so soon after his public divorce. Five years had already passed, but several failed relationships since made him more wary about being in a relationship in public. Layla tried to understand, but she was soon running out of patience.

"Ms. Little, I placed the centerpieces on each of the tables as you requested. Is there anything else that you need?" The tall male assisting her watched as Layla perused the room with her eyes hastily.

"No. No. This is fine. Thanks again for all of your help, Deacon." Layla took a deep sigh of relief and steadied herself for the entrance of the guests. She had waited for this moment and hoped that it would be glorious and victorious as she promised Leon.

Thunderous sounds of music began bellowing throughout the room. DJ Quikster, also known as Buttalove in other settings, was playing both rhythmic and slow 80s tune. Leon was pretentious in many ways, but Layla was not going to have dry church music at a joyous celebration even if Leon insisted. He compromised with 80s music; his only vice.

Guests trickled into the large conference room for the upcoming festivities. Leon's mother and sister traveled from Southern California to attend. They were staying at Leon's house in Mesa for the duration of their trip. He drove them along with his younger brother, Joseph, to the party. Layla also invited all of the church members and even some of her own co-workers. She wanted the evening to be special and subconsciously wanted Leon to recognize her efforts to treat him the way that he always longed to be treated by a woman.

When Leon entered the room with his family, he greeted Layla with a formal handshake and continued welcoming the other guests. He ignored Layla's overture for a kiss and hug, which sorely disappointed her. When he was finished welcoming each guest, Leon proceeded to the right side of the room and grabbed the microphone from DJ Quikster.

"Ladies and Gentlemen and distinguished guests..." Leon was referring to Dr. Martin Jacob Johnson, his mentor and former head pastor who encouraged Leon to enter the ministry at a young age and to attend divinity school. Dr. Johnson, his wife, and three children sat quietly in a table near the front. "Without you and especially Dr. Johnson, who has been an inspiration, I would not have my doctorate and my purpose in life. I love being a pastor. Jesus brought me through. Can I get an Amen?" Amens echoed haphazardly and joyously as if it was a Sunday morning and the now-christened Dr. Leon Blackman was preaching at his pulpit at the First Conservative Baptist Church of the Valley like he did every Sunday for the past thirty-two years. "Ya'll, we have some good food catered from Bubba's BBQ. I'm gonna bless the food first..."

Leon prayed over the food in his typical booming voice which echoed throughout the conference room. Everyone's heads were bowed except Layla, who looked glaringly at Leon as he prayed. She bowed her head and closed her eyes before he finished praying. After blessing the food, Leon escorted his mother and sister to the food table. They were the first in line. Layla watched in dismay. She shortly followed with the intention of serving a plate of food for Leon and herself. When she arrived at the food table, she quickly noticed that Leon's mother had already made him a plate. Layla could hear his mother asking Leon what food that he wanted on his plate. Determined not to make a scene, instead, Layla served herself a plate of food and waited in line with the rest of the guests. After putting a few scoops of vegetables and other items on her plate, she walked to the head table and sat down at the only empty chair available next to Leon's sister, Loretta.

"The ribs and brisket are good, but this mac and cheese is dry. I've never tasted anything so strange like this," Loretta complained as she tried to daintily spit out the food in her mouth into a napkin. She glanced towards Layla with subtle disdain in her eyes.

Layla knew that Leon's sister hated her. Leon's mother, however, adored Layla. But it was Loretta's approval that Leon needed before formalizing any relationship, especially one that was supposedly destined for marriage. Because that approval was currently withheld by Loretta, Layla knew that marriage was out of the question at this point. She feared that this obstacle may be insurmountable.

"Try the greens. They are to die for. Just like my momma's." Layla tried to deflect as quickly and politely as possible.

Loretta restrained herself from making the derogatory remark that first came to mind. After all, it was her brother's graduation party.

"I think I will." She smiled devilishly. Layla was relieved.

As the evening progressed, couples arose from their tables and began dancing on the dance floor. Layla looked around pleased. She then glanced towards Leon who seemed uncomfortable when their eyes met.

"Momma, you want to dance?" Leon asked as he turned towards his mother on his left.

"Yes, dear." Leon's mother leaped to her feet and they proceeded to the dance floor. As the song continued to the next, Leon now danced with a lovely young widow, Maya. He grasped her small waist tightly and vigorously. He smiled and darted a look deeply into her eyes. Maya was consumed as if this was her first dance ever. Her heart quickened. Leon secretly hoped that Layla could hear the widow's pulsating beat from where Layla was sitting. He always enjoyed making her jealous and letting her know that they were not yet a couple and his options were still open.

Layla, infuriated, said to the guests seated at the head table, "Excuse me. I'll be right back." She walked outside and did not bother to turn around to see Loretta's amused expression.

PIGEON PARK

OLD SAN JUAN, PUERTO RICO

Same Day

WHEN THE COUPLE reached the Chapel of Christ the Savior (which is known as *Capilla del Cristo*), they asked a local male to take a picture of them in front of the chapel with its exposed bell tower. Layla and Daniel stood joyfully arm in arm in front of the modest, stone structure; its wrought iron gate enclosed the silver and gold altar. After thanking the man for taking their picture, Layla noticed that dozens of silver ornaments decorated the inside of the chapel.

"What are those things hanging inside?" Layla inquisitively asked. As she looked closer, she could tell that some of the ornaments were various body parts - an ear, a nose, a foot, an arm, a leg. Other ornaments were of the entire body.

"I have no idea. We'll have to find out." Daniel had not yet learned of the story of the young horse rider who was miraculously saved at the location where the chapel was later built or the reason for its construction. The ornaments were placed there for those seeking miracles for physical ailments.

Within seconds of finishing his comments, Daniel's feet were inundated with three pigeons who were eager to be fed. He heard the cooing of more pigeons from afar and looked to his right towards *Parque Las Palomas*. He could see what looked like hundreds of pigeons on the ground. Some pigeons were also nestled in square holes in the reddish brick and mortar wall along the back of the park.

"Wow, this park reminds me of St. Mark's Square in Venice. Do you mind if we go in? You aren't afraid of pigeons, are you?"

"No, silly." Layla was anxious to experience Pigeon Park having never been to Italy. She had always wanted to visit the holy city of Rome. Although she could easily afford a trip to Rome and the flight from New York wasn't too long, Layla wanted to share the experience with a romantic partner. Unfortunately, none of her suitors since her divorce measured up. She secretly hoped that Daniel may be the one who she could finally feel comfortable taking to Italy. Only time would tell.

Daniel paid the two dollars so that he and Layla could enter the park. He then purchased some pigeon food from an old lady seated near the entrance of the park. He handed the bag of bird food to Layla. "Here, so you can feed them. Just watch out. They may land on your shoulder and give you a little gift." He laughed.

"You're kidding me, right?" Layla asked while wincing her eyes in concern.

She tossed some bird feed on the ground. The pigeons near her greedily ate them. Others came closer to share in the feast, hoping that the latest park guest would throw some food in their direction. Layla eagerly complied until all of the food was gone.

After a while, the birds were a little overwhelming. Realizing this, Daniel took Layla's hand and led her to the grassy area further into the park away from the crowd. They stood near the small, southern brick fence overlooking San Juan Bay facing the water. A cool breeze flushed their faces. Daniel stood directly behind Layla, nearly pressing up against her body. He pointed towards the horizon. "In the distance, there, you can see the Bacardi Distillery on the other side of the bay."

"Oh, we should go," Layla exclaimed.

"Yes, we will once we go to the Dorado area. I've never toured the facility." Layla was excited that they had another adventure on their list of things to do together.

While still looking towards the bay, Daniel slowly grabbed Layla's waist and swayed her body with the wind. She could hear him humming a song while he gently caressed her hips ever so slightly with the tips of his fingers. She could not make out any words.

"When I hold you..."

Daniel mouthed the words but sang them silently in his mind.

"When I touch you..."

He continued to sway Layla's body with his hands. Their bodies swayed in unison rhythmically. Daniel turned Layla's sensual body around so that they were face to face. He could feel her feminine warmth unmistakably. The silent sound of a sultry saxophone resounded in the song that was ringing inside of his mind. The saxophone inspired him to boldly press even closer to Layla's body. His manhood was erect and firmly pressed against her body. He could feel Layla's warmth exuding from between her firm thighs.

"When I kiss you..."

Daniel closed his eyes, cupped Layla's chin with his right hand and lifted it gently towards his mouth as he leaned his head down so that he could kiss Layla's succulent and full lips. Layla also closed her eyes in anticipation of their first kiss. She had waited for this kiss for nearly six years. As Daniel was about to suck on Layla's lips for another kiss, she pulled away from his grasp.

"No, please," she nervously said.

Daniel opened his eyes and could see and feel Layla's outstretched hand with her index finger pressed against his lips so that he could not continue. Her eyes sheepishly looked towards the ground.

"What's wrong, sweetheart?"

"I'm not... I'm not ready," Layla sighed deeply and somewhat ashamed.

"I don't understand. Is it me?"

"It's not you, Daniel. You've been a perfect gentleman. It's me. I'm sorry to say that. I'm just not ready."

"I understand." Daniel resisted the desire to pull away like a man scorned. Instead, he held Layla tightly. This comforted her. "It's okay, sweetheart. We can wait as long as you want. And if you never feel..."

"It's not that. It's that my last relationship was..."

"Do you mean Leon?"

"Yes."

Layla knew that Daniel was aware of her relationship with Leon. She had posted about their relationship on Facebook for several years. As mutual high school friends, Daniel could see all about Layla's seemingly happy relationship with Leon on Facebook except the tragic end. Layla never posted why the relationship ended abruptly. But prior to coming to Puerto Rico, she told Daniel the truth about the failed relationship. Unfortunately, not all of it.

"I just... It's that he hurt me more than any man. I was at the lowest point in my life."

Daniel listened attentively. He could see the pain in her eyes. "It's okay. If you don't feel comfortable right now talking about it, we can do something else." He wasn't sure if smiling or showing some expression of happiness in spite of the circumstances would be appropriate. He simply wanted to be reassuring.

"No, I want to tell you all of it. I'm just not sure if I should tell you now."

Layla paused.

"I... I..."

"It's okay, babe." Daniel held both of her hands and squeezed slightly.

THE CHOKIN' KIND

GILBERT, ARIZONA

Same Night, Three Years Earlier

As Layla stood under the moonlit stars trying to calm down, she could hear DJ Quikster from inside the conference room. "Boggie down, y'all. This is the Quikster aka Buttalove. I know you guys have been sweating like dogs because of tonight's grooves. The playas gotta take a break, but I'll let my tunes play so y'all can keep boogieing. Thanks for the love. I'll be back in fifteen minutes. I'm out."

Until DJ Quikster made his recent announcement, Layla hadn't realized that she had been standing outside of the building alone for nearly an hour. The time had passed quickly. She realized that this was her party. She was the hostess and needed to get back inside so that no one would be offended, especially Leon's mother, not to mention his obnoxious sister, Loretta. But before Layla mustered the courage to return to the graduation party, she could hear footsteps slowly approaching her.

"Layla... Layla, is that you?" Leon's voice was quiet yet stern.

"Yes," she said nervously when he finally came close to the light and she could discern his features. He was surprised to find her outside rather than mingling with the guests or seated at the head table with his mother and sister.

"I couldn't find you inside once the DJ took a break. How long have you been out here?" he asked.

Layla knew that Leon was too busy flirting and dancing with other women to notice that she had been gone for a long time. She quickly replied, "Only a few minutes. I had to get something out of the car." She hoped that Leon's sister would not mention her absence to him until after the party. Layla did not want to address her feelings now. She wanted to wait until they were alone, and his family had returned to California.

Leon approached closer and stood next to her. He unexpectedly grabbed her arm tightly and was about to scold her like he typically did when he was upset.

She interrupted him. "I have a gift for you, honey." She pulled a small, wrapped package from her Louie Vuitton purse and gave it to him.

"What's this?"

"It's a surprise. I hope you like it." She knew Leon hated surprises.

He looked puzzled towards it and reluctantly took it from her. Once the gift was unwrapped, Leon could see the stainless steel TAG Heuer watch; its blue dial shimmering from the outdoor lighting. He put it on.

"Thank you, dear." He quickly kissed her on the cheek. It was a small peck. The ones strangers give as greetings.

"Do you like it?"

"Yes, I do." He secretly hoped that it was a Rolex once he could tell it was a watch box in his hand, but he tried to hide his feelings. Layla could tell.

"What's wrong?"

"Nothing. I swear nothing."

"This has been a horrible day. The worst day ever," she exclaimed with derision. She could no longer hold her feelings inside.

"Now listen, lady. My mom and sister are inside, and I don't want you making a scene."

"I'm not making a scene. I'm telling you how I feel."

"You and your feelings. I'm not having it tonight. Of all nights."

"It's just that I spent five thousand dollars on your graduation party, not to mention your gift. I planned the whole thing without your help, without your family's help. We should have entered the party together as a couple. You should have introduced me to the guests and thanked me for throwing you this party when you gave your speech. You acted as if I didn't exist."

"I know you want to be my First Lady, but that's not happening yet. You know that. We talked about it already." His voice was exasperated.

"When is it going to happen? Do you even want it to happen?"

"I told you. The last woman I dated had to be admitted to a mental hospital. And my ex-wife cheated on me. I'm not gonna rush into something right away. You know that, Layla." He paused as if to collect his thoughts. "I have concerns about you. You have mental issues too."

After seeing Layla's facial expression suddenly change, Leon realized that he slipped and said something that had been on his mind, but which he had hidden from Layla whenever she asked about his concerns about their relationship.

"Mental issues? You really think that? How dare you!"

"I don't want my congregation getting used to you and then we have a public breakup. You know how I am about my reputation. I don't need anyone sullying it."

"You don't care about your reputation when you have me spend the weekend at your house when I visit from New York. The members know where I stay when I'm in Arizona. They can figure out that we were having sex, that you were fucking me all this time. Don't kid yourself, Leon."

"What did you say?" Leon's nostrils flared angrily. His eyes bulged like they were going to come out of their sockets. "I told you never to speak to me that way again." His two hands grasped her neck tightly. Layla could feel her throat tightening. She was slowly unable to breathe.

"Stop. Stop," she gasped. "I can't breathe. You're hurting me."

Leon loosened his grip. He squeezed so tight that he left bruises on her neck. He could care less about her physical or emotional well-being. His numb facial expression revealed that to her.

"My family is here. Don't start this again." He tightened his grip to emphasize his point and then pushed her aside. He took a deep breath, straightened his suit jacket, and walked away, back into the conference room.

When he was in the center of the room again, he exclaimed, "Hey ladies. Pastor Leon is back..." He lifted his arms triumphantly and smiled to the roar of the crowd.

Layla sobbed quietly so that no one could hear her. A few tears escaped despite her valiant efforts to hold them back. She tried perilously to compose herself, but her broken spirit weakened at times. It was at these moments when her true character wanted to reassert itself, but she would not let it. She fought harder and wiped away her tears in a defiant manner until the strong, relentless Layla surfaced.

There was no point returning to the party. She suspected that Leon bruised her neck in the same manner when he last assaulted her. She had no scarf to wrap her neck and to hide the markings. Given the hot Arizona evening, a scarf would be suspicious, especially because no one had seen her enter the party with any scarf on. She decided to drive back to her extended stay apartment that she rented after moving to Arizona for her job. When she finally found the keys to her Acura MDX after fumbling through her purse, she walked resolutely to her SUV.

"That was the last time, motherf$#@&," she muttered to herself as she drove away.

THE BUTTERFLY CAFE

OLD SAN JUAN, PUERTO RICO

Same Day

INSIDE THE LIGHT purple and white exterior of the Spanish colonial mansion located on *Calle de la Cruz*, Layla sat at an antique bronze metal table. The table and all of the four matching metal chairs had an intricate butterfly design. This butterfly design was consistent with the establishment's theme, which was formerly known as The Butterfly Cafe. The cafe part of the business had long been phased out. But the shop still sold beautiful arrays of exotic butterflies of all hues that were mounted on the walls inside Lucite boxes of various sizes.

Layla sat quietly at the table alone. She was somewhat despondent after the unsuccessful first kiss with Daniel in Pigeon Park. She contemplated why she reacted that way to him despite how kind and loving Daniel had been to her. Unpleasant visions of Leon circled her mind. She tried desperately to drown them out with positive emotions, especially those involving Daniel and their new-found relationship.

Layla looked up and could see Daniel standing across the room next to a large display of purple and bluish butterflies arranged in a unique layout. Darker brown butterflies were sparsely placed as accents. Daniel looked inquisitively at the piece. An older, white female proprietor approached him.

"This is beautiful," Daniel said with an odd sense of glee to the owner. "Are the butterflies local ones?"

"Some are, but most are from Brazil." Daniel was surprised by her answer. "My husband and I have been bringing them to Puerto Rico for over thirty-five years."

Although Layla was not personally involved in the conversation, she listened attentively. Besides her and Daniel, no other patrons were inside the shop.

"I especially love these blue and purple butterflies. They are amazing," Daniel mused as he pointed to a certain area of the Lucite box.

"Yes, they are." The female owner began to explain to Daniel the meaning of a blue butterfly. "The displays in my gallery do not have any pure blue butterflies. People have a diverse view of what a pure blue butterfly symbolizes. They are often seen as a sign of life. Some people believe that a butterfly symbolizes change or rebirth, regardless of its color. More importantly, pure blue butterflies are often considered a symbol of love."

The female owner looked over to Layla and smiled. In turn, Layla blushed.

She continued, "Because of their deep, vibrant colors, blue butterflies send out vibrations of joy and happiness. People respond positively when they see one or hold one in their hand. It can calm you down or help you meditate. Due to the pure blue butterfly's rarity, seeing one is a symbol of luck. There are some on the island. That's what I've heard, but I've never seen one myself."

It was a lot for Daniel to take in. "Thank you, I appreciate that."

"You're welcome. Here's my card. If you would like a special arrangement for you and your wife, just give me a call. My husband and I can design something unique just for the two of you. The cost includes shipping to the mainland."

Daniel wanted to correct her and let the owner know that he and Layla were not married, but he did not want to be rude. He also wanted Layla to ruminate on the thought that a perfect stranger considered them a married couple, especially since the owner had been married so long. Daniel considered that he and Layla made a good couple after all. He only hoped that Layla felt the same way. Part of him now had doubts about Layla's feelings towards him.

For years, Daniel secretly fancied Layla. He never told her about his feelings because he later learned that she was with Leon at the time. After that relationship broke up, Daniel was reticent to pursue Layla. When they reconnected a few years later, he told Layla that he was interested in her and that he wanted to pursue her. Daniel was pleasantly surprised when she accepted his invitation to vacation in Puerto Rico with him. He hoped that this meant that she felt the same way towards him. Subconsciously, he was now concerned that his recent overture in the park to kiss Layla may have been too soon for Layla's liking.

"Come on, honey. This is a fascinating place. I'm glad that you found it." He walked towards the table where Layla was seated.

"I wasn't really trying. I just stumbled upon it." Layla was always astonished at how upbeat and positive Daniel was about her. He frequently said little things that he liked about her or he would lavish her with comments about how beautiful and sexy she was. This was in vast contrast to how Leon treated her. Leon took every conceivable opportunity to deride her or belittle any mistake that she made. Daniel was a refreshing alternative.

But Layla was suspicious of Daniel's genuineness and wondered if it was an act. She was waiting for the true "Daniel" to finally show through. *"He couldn't be this good to me always."* She worried that, once she gave him her heart, Daniel would take it for granted and take advantage of her like most men in her past.

Part of Layla's concern was that Daniel was five years her senior. They went to the same high school, but Daniel had already graduated when Layla started there. She grew up across town and never lived near Daniel's childhood home on Chambers Lane. She never knew him personally when she was younger, but only through his reputation in high school.

Years later, when Layla joined their high school alumni club on Facebook, she also saw that Daniel was a member. She would see his infrequent posts and presumed that he saw her posts as well. Because they attended the same high school, it was expected that every alumnus would also send a personal friend request on Facebook to other alumni. So, when Daniel sent her a friend request, Layla was not surprised. They had at least four hundred Facebook friends in common.

When Daniel liked her profile pictures or commented about how beautiful she looked in the pictures that she posted on Facebook, Layla was secretly concerned. Unbeknownst to Daniel and most of their mutual Facebook friends, Layla was dating Leon at the time. She wanted the relationship to be public, but Leon did not. Daniel's comments were innocent and polite, but a part of her suspected that there was a deeper attraction behind his words. Layla never acted upon them. She was a loyal woman and would never cheat on Leon despite his maltreatment of her. She suspected that Leon was cheating on her, perhaps not sexually. She refused to believe that in part because of her ego and complete faith in her sexual prowess. She suspected that he was secretly going on dates with other women when she was home in New York. She thought that he may have dated some of the women from his church. But she had no solid proof of this, just a woman's intuition.

Because Daniel's initial interest in Layla started when she was dating Leon, she always felt guilty about it. Now that they finally kissed, Layla regretted it. She feared people might think that Layla was unfaithful to Leon when they were dating. *"Leon will definitely accuse me of cheating on him with Daniel if he ever finds out."* That thought haunted her mind and ruined the moment of their first kiss.

BRYANT PARK

MANHATTAN, NEW YORK

Three Months Earlier

"Yes, sir. He is seated over there." The young hostess pointed to a tall, stocky black male seated on the opposite side of the dining area at a table nearest to the restroom. The black male was looking down at his phone and nervously texting a message. He had not seen his lunch partner, Roland Lark, when he arrived at the Bryant Park Grill. He was too preoccupied with something else and did not look up.

"Thank you," Roland responded. He then proceeded to the table wearing khaki cargo shorts and a blue sports T-shirt. His attire was barely acceptable for the establishment. Roland did not care for the fancy Parisian-style restaurant, but his guest, Darren Meredith, insisted that, if they were going to meet in person for a discussion, then it had to be a restaurant of Darren's choosing.

Darren didn't hear Roland approaching because he was still

enthralled in responding to text messages. "That bastard," Darren unknowingly said aloud to his own surprise.

"Excuse me!"

Darren looked up startled. "No, not you, Roland. Hold on." Darren finished reading the text with disgust and voraciously typed a snide reply. "Sit down. Twenty minutes late. My time is precious. You're the one who wanted to speak to me."

"I know. I know. I'm sorry for making you wait. This is important to me. I really need your advice."

"Order the risotto with octopus and fava beans. I insist. It's to die for." Roland knew that he had to oblige; otherwise, Darren would not be cooperative for the rest of their time together."

"Sounds yummy." Roland was lying but he knew that Darren didn't care so long as he obliged. "What are you eating?"

"Me? Please. A girl has to lose weight. Water is just fine." Darren tried to hide his obvious big belly which was leaning against the table.

"Then why insist that we meet here?"

"If I am going to do this, then it might as well be in a nice atmosphere."

A loud ding emanated from Darren's phone. He glanced at this phone and ignored it so that he could get the important conversation with Roland started as soon as possible.

"So, it's been three years. What's on your mind?" Darren asked inquisitively.

"Girl problems," Roland said with a sense of shame. He always spoke to Darren when he needed advice, especially relationship advice. Today was no different.

"Honey, you came to the right hen. Tell mama your problems." Darren was eager to rekindle this aspect of their relationship.

Roland was hesitant. "I don't know where to start."

"The beginning always works for me. What's her name?"

"Layla... Layla Little"

"Beautiful name. Does she live in the city?"

"No, she has a house in Middletown."

"Being a homeowner is nice. And what does she do?"

"She's a nurse at a hospital in Poughkeepsie. I forgot the name of it."

"Wait a minute. You know my view of nurses. We talked about this before. Party girls. They are always in trouble with all that free time. Wish I could have four days off a week. Please, a girl still needs her beauty rest." Darren used his hand to fan his face, apparently indicating how hot he was. Roland smiled. Darren's antics always seemed to relax him. Today, it was welcome.

"She's not that type of woman. She's a cardiac ICU nurse. Her job is so stressful. She doesn't have time to cheat. Layla spends it with her family when she's not working."

"Crumb snatchers? You got to be kidding me. You've never dated a woman with children before. Young and dumb. That's your type. Layla must be drop dead gorgeous."

Roland pictured Layla's curves. They were in all the right places; large breasts to make a man cry for his mother, a rump that shook when she salsa danced, but her eyes. Her eyes. Layla's eyes were a deep brown; kind and gentle. The type of eyes that hide immeasurable hurt and disappointment and, instead, exude loving kindness the way that every man secretly desires, but most do not deserve. Roland almost lost himself in thinking of Layla. He resisted that temptation and refocused.

"It's not just her looks, Darren. I mean. I'm definitely not complaining. She's a looker. I like her because she is a wonderful woman and has the personality that I need." Roland knew that Layla was most of all kind and soft-spoken; the type of woman that a man would bring home for his parents to meet.

"Yes, but does she need your personality?" Darren knew Roland's reputation for being a player.

Before Roland could answer, a short redhead approached the table. "Good afternoon gentlemen. Are you ready to place your order?" Roland still couldn't get used to New York accents after all this time living there.

"Don't bother asking, hun. He's having the risotto with a glass of red wine. I'm fine with the water."

The waitress rotated her head to the right towards Roland to confirm. He nodded in the affirmative and tucked a napkin on his lap. "Can you also bring some bread?" Roland politely added.

She scribbled their order on her pad and walked off nonchalantly.

Roland felt somewhat ashamed that a grown man let another man order for him. But Roland was used to it. He had known Darren Meredith since he first moved to New York from California about a decade ago. They were an odd couple of sorts. Despite living in Los Angeles, Roland never had any gay friends before Darren. They met when Roland inadvertently stumbled upon a gay bar in Hell's Kitchen. Roland was lost and the adroit Darren instantly knew. Darren summoned Roland to his table at the rear of the bar where he was seated with several other gay men. Roland did not know why he took the chance, but he walked towards Darren and stood by his table. They hit it off and were friends ever since. The three-year dry spell was a result of Roland living with a young woman whom he met while working who did not approve of Darren's lifestyle.

"So, what's the issue, Roland?" Darren wanted to get directly to the point.

"I'm still living with Flor, but I want Layla."

Darren took a sip of water and afterward placed the tall glass down to his side so that it wasn't blocking his view of Roland. "Child, make up your mind. Do you want Layla? Or do you want Flor? Please, I bet Layla doesn't even know you are living with Flor."

"No, she doesn't." Roland looked down at the table, ashamed. He knew what was coming.

"And you're afraid that if you tell Layla about your living arrangements that she will never want you! Am I right? Child, you know it's true. Please believe. OK." Darren snapped his fingers twice for emphasis.

"I... I..."

"You gotta frog in your throat? Spit it out. Momma's waiting." Darren took another sip of water and glanced intensely at Roland. He was always impatient and today was no different.

Roland knew that, once he said the words aloud, he would have to act on it. Darren would make sure of that now that the two reconnected. "I love Flor, but I'm not in love with her anymore. Things just aren't working out and I want to give Layla a chance."

"You know what's better than pussy?" Darren asked, not expecting a response.

"What?" Roland waited anxiously for the answer.

"New pussy! Child, I know you really love Flor. Before you go messing up any relationship with her, make sure you just aren't acting on a whim because she hurt you and you're too prideful to admit it and let her know. She's been willing to overlook your silly habits so far. God knows why. I don't. Give it a chance. After you do, if it doesn't work out, then end it completely. Flor deserves that. Give yourself some time to heal before you jump into another relationship. If Layla is half the person that you say she is, then she will understand. Otherwise, dump her. And dump her fast."

After a deep sigh, Roland realized what he had to do, and that Darren was right. "We need to do this again," he said.

Darren rolled his eyes and refrained from making a quick quip. Instead, he smiled and took another sip of water.

MISSING YOU

TEMPE, ARIZONA

One Month After the Graduation Party

Layla had spent most of the early morning finishing the most time-consuming part of making her grandmother's gumbo recipe. She long-since learned that the secret to a good gumbo was making the *roux*. She learned never to rush the process because a good *roux* should develop a deep, robust flavor which forms the base of a tradi- tional seafood gumbo. The yellow onions, bell peppers, and celery had already been chopped earlier in the day. Andouille sausage would be added to the gumbo solely for flavor. Layla would not eat it. She had been a vegan for a year at that point but decided that her love for food outweighed her strict veganism. Layla's decision to become a vegan was more for health reasons anyway rather than a sense of indignation over the mistreatment of animals. Although a vegan diet was fulfilling, Layla loved eating meat. So, she compro- mised by becoming a pescatarian and supplementing her meals with fish. The shrimp and snow crab needed for the recipe were fine.

The smell of garlic, thyme, and bay leaves, as well as Cajun seasonings, filled the confines of her cozy apartment. It was near the Tempe Marketplace along the Loop 202 freeway. Although there were plenty of nice restaurants at that shopping center, Layla preferred to cook a homemade meal. It reminded her of home and her youth in California when her relatives gathered for the holidays. Besides, since the night of Leon's graduation party, Layla was despondent. She had not seen Leon or attended his church on Sunday since that day. At least a month had passed. Cooking helped soothe her soul and she knew that she needed more relaxation, now more than ever.

Her sleep was often interrupted with repeated nightmares of Leon's hate-filled eyes. She could still feel his warm breath pressing upon her like an invisible cloud of evil. Each nightmare ended with Layla gasping for air because her esophagus would actually constrict on its own, a subconscious reminder of Leon's violation. After waking from her nightmare every night, she would sob uncontrollably until she somehow cried herself back to sleep.

Layla added the Worcestershire sauce to the large metal pot. She then turned the knob on the gas stove to the right so that it was set to high heat. She waited patiently for the gumbo to boil. Once it started to boil, she reduced the heat to low so that the gumbo would simmer and the flavors meld together. Then she started making brown rice. It was a healthy alternative to white rice that she also started eating once she became a vegan.

When her iPhone rang, Layla was startled. She wondered who was calling her. She walked from the kitchen to her living room to get her purse on the nightstand. Inside was her iPhone. As she glanced inside her purse, she could see that a picture of Leon appeared on her iPhone screen. It was an old black and white picture of a young Leon in his sailor's uniform when he was in the Navy. Leon emailed her the digital picture after Layla requested it. He often mentioned serving on a guided-missile destroyer right after graduating from high school. Tales of his trips to Okinawa, Guam, Midway, and other

South Pacific islands were often used to regale his guests, especially women including Layla. Leon seemed to relish those military days before he entered the ministry. However, he rarely mentioned that he was just a cook during those four years in the Navy. That did not deter his enthusiasm.

Upon seeing his picture, Layla was reminiscent. She hesitated because she was unsure whether she should talk to Leon. This was the first time that he called her since the frightful incident. He typically texted her. She sent the call to voicemail and walked back to the kitchen to check on the brown rice.

The phone rang again, filling Layla with dread. She ignored it this time and kept cooking but had to endure the rings until the call rolled over to voicemail. She was glad that this was not the old days when people owned answering machines but could hear as the caller left the message. She was afraid of what would happen if she heard Leon's voice. At the same time, she was curious about what message Leon was leaving for her.

Moments later, he called a third time. This time Layla could not resist. She had to answer. At least it would end the annoyance so that she could finish cooking and enjoy the gumbo in silence. Layla knew that Leon was like a dog with a bone and would not stop until he got his way. And today, his bone was talking to Layla.

"Who is this?" she said as she answered the phone and selected the speaker setting so that she could continue cooking after walking back to the kitchen.

"You know who this is. This is your man," Leon said with a misplaced sense of authority.

"Umph. What do you want? I'm busy."

Leon knew that Layla had no family in Arizona and that the only friends that she had were co-workers and some female members of his congregation. So, her comment that she was busy fell on deaf ears.

"I haven't heard from you in a while. I wanted to invite you to this week's church picnic."

"The phone works two ways, Leon." Layla knew that she was

stating the obvious. She also knew that she was speaking to a brick wall. Leon often ignored her comments about his behavior or requests to treat her appropriately, like she deserved.

"Well, are you coming?"

"I'm not ready to spend time with you. I'm not sure if I'll ever be ready."

"Why not?"

"You know why." She was surprised at his response, but that was typical Leon.

"I'm sorry, but it was your fault for making me so mad. You were acting so jealous and controlling. You nearly ruined my day and in front of my mother and sister..."

Before he could say "and my congregation," Layla interrupted him. "Leon, you choked me. Again. This is the second time. I don't know if I can forgive you this time." Layla hesitated but this was what she had been feeling for a while. She knew that she needed to be strong and tell Leon the truth.

"Bitch, please. You need me. You want me. You know you want to be a First Lady and I'm the only chance you got. No one else wants you and no one else will treat you as good as I do."

Layla believed that lie in the past. She wasn't sure if she believed it anymore or if it mattered.

"I have to go." Her voice cracked in disappointment.

"See you tomorrow, babe."

She hung up without saying goodbye. The idea of seeing Leon again disgusted her. She now saw Leon in a different light for the first time. He wasn't the wholesome pastor that she believed him to be when he first started chatting with her years ago on Facebook. He always blamed his behavior on the bitter divorce and his unfaithful wife who slept with one of the deacons. But Layla suspected that there was something more, something sinister that he was hiding. She didn't know what it was, but she feared that someday it would completely come to the fore, devouring her in the process.

RIO MAR

RIO GRANDE, PUERTO RICO

Later that Same Day

THE WHITE NISSAN Altima bolted from the off-airport rental car parking lot and took the *Avenida Los Angeles* on-ramp to reach eastbound PR-26 highway towards Carolina. They decided to forgo attending the festival and head to the hotel. The city quickly faded into the horizon as the Nissan continued to PR-66 highway towards Fajardo. Lush tropical trees lined the highway as far off as the eye could see. To the far right of the highway as the Nissan drove, a large mountain peak jetted upward in the sky nearly covered in mist. One could feel the humidity from afar simply by looking at the rugged peak in all of its majesty. After driving about ten miles, the Nissan exited the freeway and made a right turn onto PR-3. As the vehicle was exiting the freeway, Layla noticed a sign: *"El Yunque Rainforest"* with a large, white right-turn arrow.

"Are we going to the rainforest?" she asked with a sense of anticipation.

"Not today, sweetheart. Our hotel is near the base of the rainforest. We can go anytime you feel like it." Daniel smiled as he appreciated Layla's eagerness for adventure. It was one of the reasons why he wanted to bring her to his homeland.

PR-3 was a four-lane road speckled with shops, restaurants, and establishments with a Puerto Rican flair. Even the mainland fast food places like Burger King and Subway advertised their wares in Spanish on this busy road to the eastern shoreline. Endless vehicles donning the phrase *"Isla Del Encanto"* on their license plates lined each lane heading east - the same direction that Layla and Daniel were heading. Some vehicles weaved in and out of traffic, frantically honking their horns at slower drivers. In the opposite direction, a caravan of horses was being ridden hard and steady on the asphalt road until they disappeared up a side road leading to homes where locals lived. Daniel continued driving until he made a left at PR-968. The Nissan slowed as it followed the narrow, winding road uphill. Nicer new townhomes were commingled with older structures. When the vehicle finally reached the gated entrance to the Wyndham Grand Rio Mar Beach Resort and Spa, Daniel made a right turn and stopped in front of the guard post.

A young Puerto Rican woman dressed in a black uniform politely greeted them with a smile, *"Bueno. Tu nombre?"*

"My name is Daniel Mendoza," he awkwardly announced.

"Sorry, sir. I thought you could speak Spanish." She switched to flawless English easily.

"I'm Puerto Rican, but my mother never taught me Spanish." Daniel tried hard to hide his embarrassment. He dreaded having to explain his past to Layla.

"That's too bad." The guard quickly checked her computer to verify a reservation under the Mendoza name. When she found it, she opened the gate. "Enjoy your stay."

"Gracias," Daniel retorted. It was one of the few phrases he learned having stayed in Puerto Rico before.

They entered Rio Mar village and drove past the tennis center on the right which was adjacent to the Greg Norman's River golf course. They continued driving until they reached the beach resort. The vehicle stopped at the main entrance. The valet opened the driver's door, handed Daniel a ticket, and then the valet proceeded around the rear of the Nissan and opened the passenger's side door. Layla exited the vehicle in a classic, light blue Caribbean sundress. The flowing skirt and high waist accentuated her sensual and fit body. A wide brim beach hat rested comfortably on her head, still allowing the long black hair of her Creole heritage to flow with the wind. Daniel escorted Layla up the steps to the main doors. Once inside, the couple walked to the reservation desk.

"We need to check in first, but I made us an early dinner reservation. I hope you don't mind. You're probably starving. It will only be a few minutes." Daniel looked over to Layla to ascertain her approval.

Layla was pleased. She realized how thoughtful and considerate Daniel was. *"I could get used to this."* She smiled as the thought crossed her mind. Layla drew closer, placed her hand on Daniel's right arm, and rested her head on his shoulder. She kissed him on his cheek. The gesture pleased her. It also calmed Daniel's nerves, although he tried not to show them.

In the previous two months, Layla and Daniel had visited each other twice. Daniel first flew to New York for the weekend. A few weeks later, Layla visited Arizona. This was their first official vacation together. It was a test of sorts. Could they get along in an environment neither of them was intimately familiar with?

◊ ◊ ◊

SEATED at a restaurant table overlooking the garden that faced the Atlantic Ocean, the couple was finally able to rest after the morning's festivities and the long drive to the resort. The sounds of coqui echoed throughout the garden. They could be heard inside the restaurant even over the constant and rhythmic roar of the ocean. Salsa music played in the distance at the activity pool. The Palio Restaurant was nearly empty which gave the couple a feeling of exclusivity as if the restaurant was reserved solely for them.

"*Buenos Noches,*" Pedro, the waiter, said as he handed both Daniel and Layla a menu. He smiled gleamingly and explained the day's special entrees.

"Order anything you like, sweetheart," Daniel said as he gazed across the table. He wondered what Layla would order as she perused the menu.

"Look, they even have Caribbean lobster." Layla was happy that she could find a meal suited to her lifestyle amongst the various Puerto Rican fare offered at the restaurant.

"Sounds delicious. You should try it."

After Layla placed her order, Daniel told Pedro that he wanted the crab *alcapurrias* to share as an appetizer. "I hope you don't mind. I think you'll like them," he said as he turned to Layla. For himself, he ordered the *pastelon de amarillos* and *malanga* gratin. He was excited to try dishes that he never had on the mainland. Several minutes later, Pedro brought the appetizer and salutarily announced, "*Provecho.*"

The two toasted their evening together with glasses of *piña colada*. As the meal progressed, a strange, uncomfortable silence originally lingered over the table. Daniel wondered if the awkwardness was due to Layla's pensive thoughts. Layla had agreed to come to Puerto Rico with Daniel if they refrained from sexual intimacy. Kissing, cuddling, and holding hands were okay. At least, that was what Layla mentioned on the mainland before their trip. Something was gnawing at her after their first kiss today. Daniel could sense it.

"How is the lobster?" Daniel asked in hopes of getting Layla to open up.

"It's delicious. Do you want to try?" Daniel smiled and nodded. Layla took her fork, grabbed a piece of the succulent white meat, and outstretched her arm to feed the morsel to Daniel. He leaned it to take it, while Layla cupped her hand underneath her fork.

"That is good. It has a unique flavor. Milder than I expected," Daniel described in a pensive manner, the way he normally does. "I'm going to have to become a pescatarian."

Layla laughed. "I'm open-minded. I don't force my dietary preferences on anyone, including my family." *"Family."* Layla's mind fixated on that word as she spoke it out loud.

Since her divorce, she had focused on raising her children, sending them to private schools and then on to college. She had a lovely family and now had her first grandchild, Cadence. She enjoyed spending the holidays with them. But something was missing. Over the years when she was dating Leon, he refused to come to New York and spend it with her family for the holidays. His pastoral duties kept him in Arizona. That left an empty void. Layla's children brought their spouses and loved ones with them to holiday celebrations. But Layla was always alone. That thought only heightened her concern now that she was taking the next step with Daniel.

"So, what are you doing for Christmas?" she inquired. "Are you visiting your family in California?"

"I spend Christmas alone." Daniel was embarrassed to admit it. "I normally spend Thanksgiving with my family. They are overbearing so spending a lot of time with them can be overwhelming. I try to visit only once a year unless it's a special occasion like a funeral or a family reunion."

Daniel continued to wax on about different times when he visited his extended family in California. Although Layla tried to pay attention, in the back of her mind, she thought that Daniel would be free to spend holidays with her family if they were a couple or ultimately married.

"My family is very loving, Daniel." Layla waited for his expression so that she could ascertain whether his intentions towards her were serious. "Cadence would love you. She's adorable. She's very smart and is a happy baby. I raised her mother to be a happy baby as well."

Pedro interrupted and asked, "How is the meal?"

"*Perfecto*," Daniel answered with a humongous smile.

QUEENS

QUEENS, NEW YORK

Two Months Earlier

WHEN FLOR accidentally dropped the glass bottle of *sofrito* on the hardwood floor causing it to shatter, she was even more upset. In her eyes, the dinner was ruined without it because most of the Puerto Rican recipes that Flor knew how to cook required *sofrito*. She thought about going out for some Chinese fast food instead of cooking dinner but quickly dismissed that. Eating a home-cooked meal was always important to her.

Flor knew that accidents like this happened frequently because there was little room to cook adequately. Their kitchen in the small studio apartment in Elmhurst was cramped when she first moved in by herself after leaving her parents' house. When Roland moved in with her three years ago, it made things worse. They were living on top of each other. Even with both incomes, they could barely afford to pay the sixteen hundred dollar rent for the studio. Then there were the various utility bills and other expenses that come with living on your own. Moving into a one-bedroom apartment was out of the question. So, Flor had to make do for now. She started to clean the soppy green mess, worrying about her future.

Last night, Roland had unexpectedly given Flor the bad news. He lost his low-paying job at the newspaper stand. That was three lost jobs in as many months. They would now again rely solely on Flor's modest income from shining shoes at a local hotel and working a second job as a parking attendant. But what upset Flor even more was that Roland finally admitted to her that his aloofness these past few months was due to a new love interest. That was devastating.

The crashing noise from the glass bottle immediately got Roland's attention. He walked into the kitchen area to find out what happened. Roland could see the frustration in Flor's frantic, hazel eyes as she struggled to mop up the floor and pick up the broken glass.

"Let me get that," Roland said as he grabbed the dustpan and broom to make it easier to sweep up the glass.

"I can do it myself. I don't need your help," Flor quickly barked back as she picked up the glass shards with her bare hands.

She was a strong, five-foot-two Puerto Rican woman in her late twenties with no kids of her own. However, she was used to taking care of her three younger brothers while growing up. Taking care of a studio apartment was a piece of cake after raising her brothers. Or so she thought. Living with Roland was not easy, and she felt like the burden rested solely on her shoulders. To her, Roland was just an oversized child rather than an adult male in his early fifties. He could barely tie his shoes in Flor's jaded opinion. He was very little help around the apartment except for the occasional handiwork that he could accomplish if he put his mind to it.

Roland backed away as he sensed Flor's frustration growing with his involvement. Flor stood up, pulled her long flowing, wavy hair into a tight bun, and then bent down on her knees to continue cleaning. Without looking up at him, she said in a quiet defeated voice, "Can you get the chicken out of the fridge?" She might as well make

Roland useful for something because he stood arms-crossed watching her.

"Yes, sweetheart."

That was a mistake.

"Don't call me sweetheart. I'm not your sweetheart. You have someone else." The cracking voice and fiery demeanor betrayed her emotions.

The snide remark stung, but Roland knew that it was true.

"I don't have anyone else. I haven't seen her in over a month. I told you about her because I wanted to be honest with you so that we can work things out. You've always told me that you want me to be honest."

He hoped that someday Flor would appreciate his honesty as well as his desire to make the relationship better even if today she could not. Flor ignored his comments but gave him a quick look of incredulity. *"Now he is blaming me."* Roland was startled at her expression. It was as if Roland could read her mind.

Roland knew that his feeble explanations were going nowhere. He told Flor the same things last night as they lay awkwardly in bed. But his words didn't seem to console her then just like they weren't now. He started to question his decision to tell Flor about Layla in the first place. After all, Roland only had dinner with Layla once. He spoke on the phone a few times with Layla and texted her on occasion. Roland tried to reassure Flor that the relationship was an innocent mistake; one that he sincerely regretted making. But she didn't believe him.

Flor grilled Roland about Layla. Did he kiss her? Did he have sex with her? Did he have secret kids that she did not know about? Was she his baby's mama? Did he love her too? Did he plan on marrying her? Flor now felt like she never truly knew Roland and that their three-year relationship was all a lie. She needed answers; truthful answers. And she needed them now. The questions seemed to never end and made Roland feel uncomfortable.

"I shouldn't have listened to Darren." But once that thought

entered his mind, Roland could hear Darren's voice say, *"I only told you to work it out. I never told you to tell her about Layla, fool."* Darren was right. He was always right. Roland needed to rectify the situation. After all, in the past few weeks, he searched deep inside of himself for what he wanted in life.

"I want to be with you, Flor. I love you." He continued his efforts to reassure her that he was genuine.

Flor thought about how Roland needed her now that he lost his job again. Maybe he said these things simply to appease her? She wondered if things between them would be different if Roland still worked at the newspaper stand. Would he have left her for Layla after all these years? Tears started to well up in her eyes, but she fought them back. She did not want to give Roland any satisfaction that he had broken her. He hadn't. Flor would never let any man break her. She learned that the hard way.

If they stayed together as Roland suggested, then it would be on her terms and her timing. The relationship wouldn't move forward as if this never happened. That's what Roland wanted. One or two conversations is what he thought it would take to smooth everything out. But she could not forget the pain so easily. Flor knew that there would be days when everything would be alright and days when the anger and betrayal would surface. Roland would need to deal with the ups and downs if he truly wanted to be with her. Her feelings weren't going to be swept under the rug and forgotten.

BOXES AND BOXES

TEMPE, ARIZONA

Two Months After Graduation Party

THE SOUND of whirling tape unwrapping and being applied to a cardboard box filled what remained in the near-empty apartment. A black sharpie marker scribbled the word "Kitchen" in all caps on the top of the box. Layla handed the box to a gentleman who packed it into her Acura MDX. Just then, a sigh of relief. This was the last box and she was finished. Layla looked around the apartment to see if there was anything that she missed. Besides a few scraps of this or that of meaningless things, there was nothing of hers that remained. She intended on shipping her belongings back to New York in her MDX except for the few things that were necessary for her carryon bag.

Because of the recent events with Leon, Layla asked to be transferred back to her old job in Poughkeepsie. It was sudden and expected, but she knew that it was the right thing to do. Her decision to move to Arizona to be closer to Leon was a failure. He didn't appreciate her or her sacrifice. It was as if he had forgotten that he was the one who asked her to move to Arizona, to leave house and home, to leave a thriving career, to leave her family and everything that she had been familiar with for the past two decades for him. Instead of appreciating her sacrifice for the relationship, she was a nuisance, a thorn in his side that he was ashamed of. She never wanted to feel that way again, to be unappreciated, unloved.

The hurt and shame that she felt were unbearable. She knew that she was crawling home empty and spent. What would her children think? What would her close girlfriend, Jeannie, think after warning Layla not to move cross-country? What would her coworkers think when she returned? Nothing that she experienced these past few years prepared her for this. The dreams of being loved, of being desired, of being fulfilled in a relationship that she desperately longed for were now gone like voices whispering and then disappearing into thin air, never to be heard again. Her anger increased. Why did she listen to him and not Jeannie? Why did she fall in love again when she told herself not to?

She held back tears. But in reality, her eyes were bone dry because she had no more tears to give. The grief was so immense that it washed over her until the only thing that was left was hope; pure and undefiled. She knew that she could never be the same anymore, never feel love again, never be so vulnerable to a man that she could do this to herself again, allow herself to be destroyed by an uncaring and undeserving man.

He was less than a man to her now. She knew it better than she did before. She was stronger than she was ever before. How she could stoop so low, she could not answer. But she had the strength now to leave, to end it all despite her valiant efforts to make the relationship work.

With an unsteady hand at first, she gathered her purse, the keys to the apartment and the gate key, and walked out, locking the door behind her. To her, it was a physical representation of the closure that she needed with Leon. She headed to the manager's office and gave the keys to a young woman, Candace.

"I'm sorry to see you go, Ms. Little. You were an excellent tenant." Candace chose not to mention that Layla worked a lot and was never there and never complained or fussed over any issues with the apartment. "As I explained you had a few more months left on your lease. The company may bill you for at least one month's rent if we aren't able to rent the apartment."

"I understand, Candace. Thank you for explaining it again." Her half-hearted smile betrayed Layla's uncomfortableness with the situation. At least Candace was friendly.

Layla walked out of the office into the parking lot. She watched as the car-carrying trailer drove off and headed to the next destination. The trailer was loaded with her Acura MDX filled with her packed boxes and six other vehicles. A few minutes later, the Uber arrived, and the driver put her carryon bag into the trunk. Layla entered the vehicle with her purse clenched tightly.

"We should be there in about twelve minutes, ma'am," said the driver in a husky voice. "What airline?"

"Thank you." Layla double-checked the Wallet app on her iPhone for her boarding pass. "It's American Airlines, Terminal 4."

As the Uber driver sped off, Layla's phone rang. It was Leon. She ignored his call because she did not want to let him know that she was moving back to New York.

BIO-BAY

FAJARDO, PUERTO RICO

The Next Evening

AFTER PARKING the Nissan Altima in a parking spot on *Las Crobas* Boulevard in Fajardo, Layla and Daniel walked across the street and then down towards the beach. The moonlit night was gorgeous. The waves lapped gently onto the beach. It was a perfect spot to go night kayaking.

"Is Ismael here?" Daniel asked a young lady with a bull horn. A name tag was on the upper left of her white blouse. On it was the word: "Matilda."

"Yes." Matilda pointed to a gentleman a little further along the roadway near a boat ramp. A group of about twenty men and women encircled him. He was handing out life vests and helmets with what appeared to be lights connected on the top. "There he is. Follow his directions. Have a nice time."

"Thank you, ma'am," Daniel cordially responded.

Layla grabbed Daniel's hand and the two walked closer to the group.

"It's cold," Layla's shivering voice could barely be heard over the roar of the ocean and the excitement of the various individuals waiting to kayak with the tour groups assembled near the beach. Layla moved closer to Daniel in hopes of sharing his warmth. He placed his arm around her.

"I'm sorry, sweetheart. I thought the 8 o'clock tour would be nicer because it would be darker, and we could see the bio-bay better. I didn't realize that it would be cooler."

The couple joined their tour group, grabbed a vest and helmet, and listened attentively. As Ismael explained the trip to the bioluminescent bay, two rows of yellow and red kayaks lined the beach. Eventually, the kayakers entered the water with the lead kayak pointing the way. The group kayaked across the boat marina to a thin channel that led to a lagoon. Each kayak was in a single file with the occasional straggler. Novices and experts were among them. One could see arms frantically paddling to avoid hitting the other kayaks or, worse yet, the sides of the channel. Aged, lush mangrove trees intertwined to form a green and brown canopy over the entire channel. Long, odd-shaped branches were occasionally low in some areas, making the venture dangerous at times. The sound of people crying out "watch out," "be careful," and other phrases of concern filled the quiet, night air. The rustling of branches or a thud from a kayak hitting a mangrove tree would be heard shortly thereafter.

"I don't know what I'm doing." Layla grabbed the kayak paddle so tight that her knuckles whitened. She sat in front of Daniel on the kayak.

"Have you kayaked before?" Daniel asked hesitantly.

"No, this is my first time."

"Just remember what Ismael said. Keep the paddle perpendicular to the boat. Place the right side of your paddle blade in the water near your feet." Layla followed Daniel's instructions as he spoke. "Ok, like that. Now rotate your torso as you're pulling the blade through the water alongside of the kayak. Yes, like that. Retract your right arm while at the same time extending your left arm. Now do the reverse."

Daniel could see Layla's strokes and sensed that her confidence level increased. "You got it. Great."

After ten minutes of paddling through the channel, Layla asked, "How much longer? Are we there yet?"

"I don't think so. The tour book said that it takes about an hour to get to the center of the lagoon."

"You're kidding me," her voice echoed in the night air.

"But it's worth it, sweetheart. I promise you. You'll love it."

"I'm not gonna make it, Daniel," Layla's exasperated voice trembled slightly as she spoke.

"Don't worry. Bring your paddle to your lap and relax." Daniel began to take stronger strokes with his paddle so that Layla did not have to paddle anymore. As their kayak began to glide faster on the surface of the water, Daniel added, "We'll be fine. Enjoy the view." A sigh of relief could be heard from Layla.

The kayaks from their tour group continued meandering the narrow channel. It was a clear night with a new moon. The moonlight glistened through the mangroves, illuminating the waters as well as the maze of roots from the humongous trees forming the canopy. The familiar sound of coqui echoed in the distance. Iguanas sleeping in the trees were accustomed to the ruckus. Within no time, the group of kayaks navigated beyond the channel and entered the crystal waters of *Laguna Grande*. In the distance on a cliff overlooking the lagoon, the rotating beam of light from the lighthouse known as *Faro de Las Cabezas de San Juan* brightened the darkened sky, cutting it like a knife.

When the kayaks reached the center of the lagoon, Ismael used his paddle to rotate his kayak so that he faced the group. Ismael was a marine biologist who graduated from the University of Puerto Rico. "I'm glad everyone made it. You guys did an excellent job. This is a bioluminescent bay. There are five in the entire world. Puerto Rico has three of them. The red mangroves that we passed not only line the channel, they also surround this entire lagoon." Ismael's outstretched arms circled the lagoon. The visitors' eyes followed him attentively. "The roots of the mangroves release tannins. Tannins are rich in Vitamin B12, which is an important nutrient for light emitting dinoflagellates."

As Ismael spoke, he dipped his hand in the water. "The dinoflagellates burst into light when they feel pressure against their cell walls." Blue lights sparkled as he moved his hand. "You try."

The group eagerly complied. Layla and Daniel each moved their hands in the warm waters of the shallow lagoon. The iridescent sea life fascinated them. It was as if they were all alone enjoying the beautiful starlit, night sky.

"This is incredible," exclaimed Layla with a child-like sense of exuberance.

"Yes, it is. I'm glad you like it."

"It was definitely worth all of my efforts," Layla laughed as she realized how much paddling she avoided.

"We couldn't do it without you." Daniel's jovial voice also turned into laughter.

They continued soaking in the experience. After a while, the group of kayaks headed back through the channel and landed on the beach with the assistance of a crew member. Vests and helmets were returned. The group members scattered into the dark, returning to their cars and heading back to their hotels.

Layla and Daniel stayed behind, drinking in the lovely views and nocturnal sounds. They sat on a bench overlooking the beach.

"Puerto Rico is so beautiful. This was a lovely surprise." Layla was impressed that Daniel was willing to share his homeland with her and plan a romantic getaway.

"I love Puerto Rico. I wish that I was born here and lived here all my life. Maybe someday, I'll buy a place of my own not too far from this lagoon."

Daniel slipped his arm around Layla and nestled closer to her. He nibbled on her ear and gently kissed her neck. A smile touched

Layla's lips. She began to breathe deeper as Daniel continued kissing her neck with gentle pecks. She turned her head towards him, eyes aglow. She leaned in and they kissed, supple kisses the way that new lovers do; anxious and tender. Daniel cupped the back of Layla's head and played with her flowing, black hair as they kissed.

"*I want to feel like this forever,*" Layla thought. "*I need love. I deserve to be loved.*"

Layla slipped her hand underneath Daniel's shirt and rubbed his bare body. She lifted his shirt over his head and removed it. It fell to the ground. Their bodies instinctively pressed closer.

A loud ring suddenly interrupted the passion. It was Layla's phone.

As she opened her purse to answer the call, Daniel reached out and softly touched her hand. "Sweetheart, let it go to voicemail." He continued kissing her.

"No, I can't. It may be Amirah or Jasmine." Another kiss. "Please..."

"Okay." Daniel took a deep breath to still his heart and compose himself.

Layla looked at her iPhone and saw "Leon Blackman" emblazoned on the screen along with his black and white Navy photo. Her heart dropped.

◊ ◊ ◊

FURTHER UP THE road on *Las Crobas* Boulevard, a rental car was parked askew with a view of the bench where Layla and Daniel sat. The driver sat intensely watching the couple with binoculars. When he was satisfied that the interruption spoiled the couple's mood, he pushed the red button on his phone ending the call.

EL YUNQUE

RIO GRANDE, PUERTO RICO

The Next Day

LAYLA HESITANTLY APPROACHED the concierge's desk in the lobby of the third floor of the Wyndham Grand Rio Mar hotel. She was eager to plan something for Daniel because he had secretly planned the night kayaking trip at the bio bay the day before. As she approached, the male concierge smiled, revealing his deep dimples on both sides of his face.

"How may I help you, *Senorita*?" he asked inquisitively.

"When we drove here, I saw a sign for the rain forest. Is that nearby?"

"Oh yes. It's about a fifteen-minute drive from here. Are you interested in a tour? I can arrange one if you'd like?"

"No, thank you. We have a rental car and can drive there. I was interested in knowing what things I can do there."

"Let me see. I was looking at this the other day, but I want to make sure the information is still accurate." With a few clicks of the mouse, the young Puerto Rican male quickly navigated his computer to look up the status of *El Yunque* rainforest. "Oh, you know Hurricane Maria devastated the rainforest."

"Oh no. I hadn't heard," Layla nervously retorted, hoping that her plans would not be in vain.

"But parts of it have reopened. You won't be able to take the hike to *La Mina* Falls. I'm so sorry. That's such a beautiful hike. The falls are so spectacular. It's a popular place for visitors and locals to see." After a few more clicks, he continued. "But you will be able to see *La Coca* Falls. It's right by the side of the road. You just pull over and walk a few feet. It's still a nice view."

"Is there anything else we can do?"

"Well, the *Yokahu* Tower is open. It has nice views of a lot of the rain forest and even the Caribbean." He also explained that the recreational area was opened as well as *Bano Grande*. *Bano Grande* was a large, circular man-made pool built in the 1930s formed by a stone and masonry dam. The water cascaded over the dam creating the pool. Layla listened attentively. Her mind calculated what would be a romantic adventure.

"I'm sure it will be lovely. Thanks for the help."

"Anytime. Let me know if there is anything else that you need. Enjoy your day. Remember, it rains in Puerto Rico especially in the rainforest. So, you may want to bring an umbrella if you're scared of a little rain." He chuckled. "Hiking boots help but aren't required."

Layla returned his kind words with a smile. She then walked back to their ocean-view suite on the second floor of the hotel. Daniel was on the balcony enjoying the palm tree-studded view of the Atlantic and the salty air. She walked out to the balcony to relay her plans.

◊ ◊ ◊

WHEN THE DOORBELL WAS PUSHED, a petite young Puerto Rican

lady, Genesis, opened the front door to the Lluvia Deli Bar & Arte-facto, a popular dining spot for locals at the base of *El Yunque*. She showed Layla and Daniel to their seats near the outdoor patio. As Layla sat down, she noticed a few patrons who were also staying at the nearby Wyndham hotel. A Puerto Rican family with their four-year-old son in a highchair was seated in the large table adjacent to them. They spoke Spanish loud and enthusiastically like most of the deli's patrons.

Genesis handed both Layla and Daniel a breakfast menu.

"Would you like something to drink? Margaritas are two for six dollars."

Daniel looked at Layla.

"It's too early to drink," she added. Layla's mind thought of the Five O'Clock Somewhere Bar at the hotel. She quickly dismissed it. She glanced at the menu. "I would like a blackberry lemonade and some guava pancakes." Layla closed her menu and handed it to Genesis.

"And you, *Caballero*?" she asked as she glanced towards Daniel.

"Can I have the bacon waffles? And a glass of orange juice if they are in season."

"Good choice. Yes, they are in season." Genesis took Daniel's menu and placed their order.

As Genesis approached the kitchen, Layla lowered her eyes and fidgeted. After an awkward silence, Layla reached across the table and held Daniel's hand. He looked at her with some hesitation, wondering what happened to her loving demeanor after she received last night's call. Layla had been more distant since.

"Is everything alright sweetheart? Did you call Amirah back?" Daniel did not want to pry, but he wanted to show that he was inter-ested in Layla and her family and that he cared about her feelings.

"No. No. This morning I left a message for Jasmine instead. Cadence is growing so fast. I can't believe how tall she is now. Three years old already."

Layla's eyes wandered. She avoided looking at Daniel while

speaking. As an attorney, Daniel was used to this. He was familiar with how witnesses respond when lying during depositions or on the stand. But he wanted to give Layla the benefit of the doubt. If their budding relationship was going to succeed, then he had to earn her trust and suppress the desire to confront her or ask questions as if she was under interrogation.

"Jasmine, she's your oldest daughter."

"Yes, my firstborn and my heart. She's all grown up now. Her husband took a job in Florida. They've been living there this past year." Layla glowed as she spoke.

"Do you see them often?"

"No, not yet. Well, not this year. I have a new job so I'm not scheduling any vacations until I'm more secure in my job."

With two warm plates in her hand, Genesis brought the food to the table. The couple ate and continued their early morning conversation. After breakfast, they drove to the rainforest.

As THEY STOOD atop of *Yokahu* Tower's observation deck, the panoramic views of the lush and tropical *El Yunque* rainforest seemed to stretch endlessly in every direction. The turquoise waters and the southeast coast of the Caribbean were in the distance; offshore islands that encompassed the Puerto Rican archipelago could also be seen. Majestic mountain peaks jutted from both sides; the West Peak on the left and the *Los Picachos* and *El Yunque* peaks to the right. The billowing clouds covering the peaks formed their own sort of cloud forest made of whites, grays, and silvers.

A green Puerto Rican amazon, also known as the Puerto Rican parrot, flew past with a red forehead and white rings around both eyes. Its distinctive blue feathers could be seen as it wings stroked during flight. The deep blue feathers were in stark contrast to the various green hues of the rainforest. The amazon flew fast and agile until it was out of sight.

"Look, mom. I can see everything," a blond-haired, blue-eyed boy said while looking through the large aluminum viewfinder on the observation deck. When his mother never answered, the boy looked around. Not seeing her, he ran down the spiral steps to the bottom of the tower to find her. "Mom... Mom..."

Layla's eyes gazed away from the scenic views and watched as the boy descended. The couple was now alone on the tower.

Layla breathed deeply, soaking in the fresh forest air.

"Did you see the parrot?" she asked. "I wonder if the gift shop has some souvenirs of it. It was so magnificent." Layla turned around and started walking towards the stairs. Daniel followed.

"Yes, it was. I hadn't seen one before." Daniel smiled and thought of the blue butterflies. He wondered if they would be fortunate enough to see one. How would seeing a blue butterfly affect their relationship? Would it bring the luck that they desperately needed to take the relationship to the next level? Daniel knew that Layla was holding back. He did not know why but had his suspicions.

After they descended down the spiral stairs and exited the tower, Layla walked towards the gift shop. Daniel looked around and said, "Sweetheart, I'm going to take a few pictures of the tower from this vantage point. Is that okay with you? I can meet you in the gift shop in a bit."

"Sure, don't miss out," Layla said without turning around to look in Daniel's direction.

As Daniel walked around the faded pink tower, he looked for places to take a picture without any other guests who would obscure the view. He stepped backward once or twice so that the entire tower could fit into view of the camera on his iPhone. While doing so, he accidentally stepped on someone's shoe.

"Watch where you are going man," the voice bellowed from a five-foot-two male inconspicuously dressed for being in a rainforest. The male was obviously not prepared for the humid and rainy weather.

"I'm sorry," Daniel responded as he turned towards the male. Leon's expression was stern and irate when he met Daniel's eyes.

"I know who you are. You're Layla's new fling." Leon's eyes gave Daniel the once over with a sense of disgust. "Umm, another Knight. I'm not surprised. She has a thing for Lynwood boys. But she's my woman." Leon rushed towards Daniel as if to confront him head-on. His body jerked when Daniel side-stepped to avoid him.

"Listen, man. I know who you are too. What are you doing here?" Daniel's anger grew as he realized that Leon could ruin the well-planned, romantic trip. Daniel was still uncertain of Layla's feelings toward Leon despite the passage of time since their breakup three years ago. Daniel knew that Leon continued pursuing Layla despite her repeated efforts to remind Leon that the relationship was over.

"I said she's mine." Leon righted himself toward Daniel and grabbed his shirt with both hands to jerk him around.

"Get off me," Daniel yelled. He pushed the shorter Leon force-fully with both arms, causing him to stumble backward and to lose his footing. Leon fell to the ground, hitting his head on the cement walkway.

"Daniel! What are you doing?" Layla exclaimed as she quickly approached. She knelt down near Leon, embracing his head. "Are you alright?" Layla gave Daniel a dirty look and then tended to Leon.

CHANCE ENCOUNTER

NEWARK, NEW JERSEY

Earlier That Week

"ATTENTION PASSENGERS. United Airlines Flight 1102 from Newark to San Juan has a gate change from Gate 108 to Gate 132. Attention passengers..."

As the PA system for Terminal C of Newark Liberty International Airport echoed throughout the concourse, Layla raised her head and glanced at the screen near Gate 108 to confirm what she had just heard. The screen no longer showed that Flight 1102 was departing from that gate. Instead, it indicated a new departure to Chicago.

Layla stood up, grabbed her purse and carry-on luggage, and walked through the busy concourse until she reached Gate 132. Her Apple Airpods were playing the rhythmic sounds of "Love Will Follow" by Kenny Loggins as she walked.

When she reached the gate, she sat down on the metal chair bolted to the floor. She plugged the charger to her iPhone in the outlet that was on the table in front of her. Also attached to the table was a stationary and upright iPad that was equipped by the airport restaurants. Layla began perusing the iPad. She scrolled through the restaurant app until she reached the screen where she could order a glass of wine. She selected a glass of 2014 Parr Vineyard Chardonnay from Maldonado Vineyards; a small vineyard in Jamieson Canyon of southern Napa Valley. The Chardonnay was described as having complex aromas offering maple, clove spiced pear, candied lemon peel, and toasty oak. That item pleased her.

She slid her credit card in the reader attached to the iPad to pay. Using the boarding pass on her iPhone, Layla scanned it with the iPad before she could finish her transaction. The iPad confirmed that her flight to San Juan was an hour away and on-time and then it finalized her purchase. The screen informed her that the glass of Chardonnay would be delivered within five minutes.

With an hour to go before her flight, Layla tried to relax. The hour-long drive to Newark was exhausting. She was already tired before leaving to the airport. She had just completed a twelve-hour night shift at the hospital. Her wearied body was reluctantly getting used to the change from day shifts to night shifts after her ninety-day training program ended. She was looking forward to her vacation with Daniel, but not the four-hour flight to San Juan. Sleeping on a plane was always difficult for her. She hadn't slept before leaving for the airport. So she wanted to relax as best as she could while in the concourse.

Besides a refreshing drink, she needed to pass the time. Layla decided to find out how her oldest daughter, Jasmine, was doing. Layla texted Jasmine: "Princess, how is Cadence? I saw the video of her making Christmas decorations on Facebook. So cute! Will Face-Time later tonight. Luv u."

"Cadence says she loves Grammy. Love you too mom." The response seemed instantaneous.

Layla was relieved. She had worried that Jasmine would be upset that she was spending the Thanksgiving holiday in Puerto Rico with

Daniel instead of visiting her in Miami. None of her three children had met Daniel. Her son, Kalvin, was stationed in Okinawa. Her daughters, Jasmine and Amirah, no longer lived at home. So, Daniel could visit Layla without her children's knowledge. Layla was leery to introduce Daniel or any other man to her family after the failed, long relationship with Leon. She wanted to make sure that Daniel was the right fit first. The vacation together was meant to allay her fears.

From the corner of her eye, Layla could see the male server approaching with a wine glass in his hand. He looked very familiar, so she turned her head towards his direction. Roland Lark was dressed in a blue server's uniform. He paused when he recognized her face, but then continued walking towards her. He placed the wine glass on her table and handed her a napkin.

"Would you like something else?" he asked obligatorily.

"No, thank you." Layla hoped that this chance encounter would end quickly and uneventful. She was wrong.

"Layla, I... I..." Roland stammered to start the conversation. When he finally mustered the strength to do so, he continued. "I know that I wronged you. I'm sorry, Layla."

"Roland, you wouldn't take my calls or return my texts. You dropped off the face of the earth and all you have to say is you're sorry."

He could see the disappointment in her eyes despite her valiant efforts to hide it.

"I admit that you deserve better. You deserve an explanation." Roland, however, was still reluctant to tell Layla, especially at work. He hoped that he could convince Layla to talk to him on another day when they could be alone. But he knew that things were complicated.

He was still living with Flor in Elmhurst. Flor's heart had not fully recovered from his betrayal. Roland doubted that she would ever truly forgive him, but he struggled to earn her trust again. It was not an easy two months since he told Flor about Layla. Something told Roland that it may take years to repair his relationship with Flor.

That was too long for Roland's liking. Many times, Roland wanted to give up and move in a different direction. Seeing Layla seated at the table drinking white wine and dressed in a comfortable yet elegant outfit rekindled his feelings for her.

"You look beautiful. Are you going to see Cadence?" Roland knew how much Layla loved her three-year-old granddaughter. He was hoping that his interest in her would disarm Layla and allow her to open up.

"I know what you're trying to do. It's not gonna work. Shouldn't you go back to work and do whatever it is you're supposed to be doing right now?" She was frustrated by his persistence.

"I just need to talk to you." Even though he was not invited, Roland sat down on the chair next to her. Roland didn't know when he would get this opportunity again and he did not want to squander it.

"Make it quick. My flight is leaving soon." She took another sip of the Chardonnay.

"I need you Lay. I miss you. I want to see you again." His sheepish eyes were glazed over. Layla could see the sincerity in them. She wondered why he had not reached out to her before.

"It's too late, Roland. I'm with someone now. That's why I am here."

"Who is he?"

"It doesn't matter. You don't know him."

"I treat you better than he does." When Layla looked at him cross-eyed, he corrected himself. "I will treat you better than he does." His voice emphasized his new-found determination as he gently touched her shoulder. In so doing, he could sense Layla's relief as well as her profound sorrow.

"Daniel is kind to me. He believes in me. He listens to me when I speak and encourages me. And he takes my calls and returns my texts." Layla jerked her shoulder to loosen Roland's hand. He realized that she was determined despite his openness.

"Are you going to see him now?"

"It's none of your business, Roland. Please leave me alone."

Roland stood up and stepped back. He gazed up at the screen and noticed that it indicated that Flight 1102 would be boarding in twenty-five minutes, bound to San Juan, Puerto Rico.

"Ok. I'm here if you want to talk."

Layla watched as Roland silently walked off. She took a deep breath while a tear tugged loose from her eye, leaving a trail down her left cheek.

THE BEACH

RIO MAR, PUERTO RICO

The Next Morning

LAYLA REMEMBERED ENTERING the small gift shop near the entrance to the *Yokahu* Tower. Scattered throughout the gift shop were T-shirts, towels, ceramic tiles, and other knickknacks with pictures of the tower. She rifled through photos for sale, but none had any of the Puerto Rican amazon that she had hoped to buy after seeing one in flight. But in the back, behind the cash register was a poster of a blue butterfly surrounded by other multi-colored butterflies. The poster brought a smile to Layla's face as she remembered the Butterfly Cafe. Layla continued looking for a souvenir that pleased her.

Having failed in finding something that she wanted as a souvenir, Layla remembered exiting the gift shop and walking around the tower towards the area where she believed that Daniel would take a picture. Layla remembered walking closer and seeing the back of a male body whom she recognized as Leon. Thrusting forward were

Daniel's arms forcing Leon to fall back and hit the ground. Layla remembered feeling shocked when she saw Daniel behaving aggressively toward Leon; unprovoked.

Layla exclaimed, "Daniel! What are you doing?" She walked briskly toward Leon.

While she was tending to him, Leon in a gruff voice said, "Is this who you want to be with? He is a jerk. He pushed me."

"You're lying." Daniel looked at Layla to ascertain her reaction. Her eyes were empty. Daniel knew that, whatever he said, it would not matter. Leon would deny it and Layla would just take any statement as an excuse.

"Enough already. You two. I don't want to hear it. Daniel, please go away. Give me some time alone with him," Layla urged.

As Daniel walked away in disgust, he could see Leon's evil eye looking at him and feigning distress in hopes of drawing upon Layla's compassion as a nurse. Leon knew that, despite their rocky past, Layla still harbored feelings for him. She would accept his calls on occasion and sometimes return his texts. That was enough to give him hope over the years. Now that she was showing concern for him, Leon hoped things would take a turn for the better. Layla remembered the conflicting feelings that she felt when tending to Leon; feelings of compassion mixed with decreasing disdain.

Layla repeated the events of the preceding day over and over in her mind. The image of Leon hitting his head on the hard cement became more and more ingrained in her mind. She wondered, who was this Daniel? Was he just as violent as Leon? Would he treat her the same way? Should she be afraid of him? She was beginning to be afraid of him. She had second thoughts of coming to Puerto Rico and vacationing with him. Was she going too fast? Was she making the same mistakes that she made with Leon?

She lay in bed mulling over these thoughts again and again. Rustling noises and sounds of Daniel dressing and getting ready for the day filled the hotel suite. She could hear him mumbling something to himself and checking his iPhone. Lying still, she pretended to be asleep until she heard the sound of the hotel door open and then close.

Daniel walked out of the rear of the Wyndham Grand Rio Mar hotel towards the activity pool until he reached the towel shack. A young male named Jose finished pushing a large, wooden towel cart filled with beige and blue towels into place. He then laid the sign-out binder on the ledge of the shack for hotel guests to sign.

As Daniel approached, Jose said "Good morning, *Caballero*" with a strong Puerto Rican accent which indicated that English was not his first language. Daniel greeted Jose. Daniel requested a towel, which José promptly provided after Daniel gave his name and suite number. With a towel in his hand, Daniel walked around the entrance to the pool slide and then towards the beach. A sign indicated that he was leaving hotel property and entering a public beach.

Walking along the sand towards the water, Daniel saw two rows of bronze chaise lounges. Two hotel employees were using a cordless power drill to make a hole in the sand in between two chaise lounges that were paired together. They inserted an umbrella in the hole and covered the hole with sand using their feet to stabilize it. The employees walked to the next pair of chaise lounges and repeated the process.

Daniel lay down on the chaise lounge nearest to him and soaked up the view of small waves crashing onto the beach and rolling back out towards the ocean. A young boy about nine years old gleefully ran past Daniel to a pair of chaise lounges further west of him. The boy looked around at the other empty lounges as his younger brother and parents walked closer. Pointing to several chaise lounges nearby, the boy excitedly proclaimed, "I claim these chairs for me. All of them." He dropped his blue towel onto one chaise lounge and then

gleefully ran into the warm Atlantic water to play. His family
followed suit.

Daniel's eyes scoured the rest of the beach. Very few guests were
on the beach so early in the morning, so he tried to relax. After a deep
sigh, Daniel wrestled with the downward spiraling situation. He
knew Layla was upset at him for what happened with Leon. Daniel
had no idea that her fears of him were growing. A sense of hopeless-
ness rose from inside his bosom.

"*Six years. Six years. I waited six years to finally get close to her.*"
Daniel's thoughts raced. Just when he thought Layla was finally
getting over the pain of her past relationship and willing to open her
heart again, the ever-destructive Leon had placed his claws into her
again. At least, that is what Daniel feared.

He tried in earnest to rid himself of these destructive thoughts.
He remembered their first kiss overlooking San Juan bay. He remembered kayaking under the stars and how Layla passionately kissed
him and drew him nearer. Thoughts of ecstasy ensued as he re-
enacted in his mind how they almost made love on the beach while
the roaring waves echoed their beating hearts. And then it hit him. "*It
was Leon who called and interrupted us, not Amirah.*"

Daniel's anger and frustration surfaced. He wondered how long
Leon had been following them. The idea was disgusting. He
wondered how Leon found out that they were vacationing in Puerto
Rico for Thanksgiving. Did Layla tell him? She promised Daniel that
she cut off all ties to Leon and blocked his number after he continued
to belittle her and stalk her by phone. Was Layla honest about this?
Had she been misleading Daniel the whole time? Nothing seemed
right. Daniel struggled with betrayal, but he wanted to give Layla the
benefit of the doubt. Layla told Daniel about Leon's bizarre obsession
with her. He vowed never to let her go, never to let another man have
her. He loved her and no one else would be allowed to love her. The
fault had to be Leon's. Layla would not willingly give Leon another
chance. Would she?

THE SHUTTLE

RIO MAR, PUERTO RICO

The Same Morning

Around ten o'clock that same morning, Daniel was still enjoying the spectacular ocean view from the chaise lounge. As the morning progressed, kite surfers and kayakers started harnessing the wind and the waves. A brown pelican flew low over the aqua blue waters; its head held back on its shoulders and its bill resting on its folded neck. For a moment, Daniel thought it would dive and submerge completely below the surface of the water to capture a fish. Instead, the pelican continued flying until it could no longer be seen.

Earlier, Daniel had received a call from the receptionist of his law firm letting him know that the firm received a new lawsuit. The new case involved the tragic fall down the steps by a young mother at a Scottsdale hotel in Arizona. He had already called the general manager of the hotel and even spoke to their in-house counsel about the new lawsuit. Emails and texts were also exchanged. By the time he handed the immediate reins of the case to a younger associate attorney, Daniel was ready to escape the unfortunate interruption and focus again on his vacation and on Layla.

Layla hadn't woken up when he left the hotel room. He did not want to wake her up to tell her that he needed some quiet time to think and that he was going to lay out on the beach. He also regretfully remembered that he forgot to leave a note letting Layla know where he was. Calling her cellphone earlier in the morning was out of the question. Layla arrived at the hotel room really late that night after the incident with Leon. Daniel did not want to disturb her when he first started relaxing on the chaise lounge. Figuring that she might just be waking up by now, Daniel decided to text her his location on the beach. He hoped that this would allay her concerns when she woke up and did not see him there. She did not immediately respond. So, he let it go.

A male waiter, Emmanuel, was greeting the few guests scattered on various chaise lounges situated on the beach. In his hand were menus from the Five O'Clock Somewhere Bar & Grill. The tiki-style bar was beachside, only a stone's throw away from the sunbathers. After giving other guests menus to peruse, Emmanuel reached Daniel's chaise lounge.

"Good morning, boss. Would you like anything?" the waiter said enthusiastically.

Daniel reached out his hand for a menu and Emmanuel obliged. Only looking for a light meal, Daniel ordered the fish tacos with *malanga* fries and iced lemonade.

"Boss, I'll be back with your drink in a moment, but the fish tacos will take about ten or fifteen minutes. Ok."

Daniel nodded and handed back the menu. Emmanuel cheerfully walked away to the next guest to take their order. Just then, Daniel's iPhone buzzed. It was a text from Layla: "I'll be down in a minute." A curt "Ok" was his response. He was hesitant to type more.

Daniel's heart palpitated so fast it almost jumped out of his body. He became so nervous that sweat dripped down his forehead profusely as if they were tears instead. Using the beige towel, he wiped them off. He wanted to look calm and presentable when Layla arrived. Daniel second-guessed ordering the iced lemonade. Perhaps something stronger was necessary, but Emmanuel was nowhere in sight.

◊ ◊ ◊

As Daniel took steps forward, the wet sand beneath his feet sunk an inch or more. His footprints faded as the waves washed the sand away, causing the sand to tumble turbulently inside the waves and dissipate into the bowels of the endless ocean. The warm Atlantic waters covered Daniel's feet just past his ankles as he walked. He dared not walk too far along the mile-long stretch of beach lest Layla missed him and assumed the worst.

When he headed back to the pair of chaise lounges where he had been relaxing all morning, Daniel saw Layla enter the beach from the resort. A beach bag hung from her right shoulder and oversized, square sunglasses shielded her eyes. She walked gracefully towards the ocean and where Daniel had described his location. By the time Daniel approached her, she had almost reached the pair of chaise lounges. After seeing Daniel's belongings, Layla placed her beach bag on the side of the chaise lounge and then looked towards Daniel.

"Good morning." Hesitation was in her voice.

"Good morning, sweetheart." The last word stuck in his throat; not because he had lost any feelings for her. Perhaps, he did. But because he was leery of her reaction and concerned that she had closed off any emotional connection with him that they had developed over the past few months. "Are you hungry? I ordered fish tacos." He hoped Emmanuel would quickly return with the food so that the shared meal would serve as both a distraction and a sorely needed bonding experience.

"No, I lost my appetite."

"Ok." Daniel sensed that Layla had something on her mind;

something she wanted to discuss with him. He backed off to give her space to raise the issue.

Layla lay down on the chaise lounge and fidgeted until she was comfortable. She grabbed a book from the beach bag and began reading. Daniel relaxed next to her. He wanted to offer to rub suntan lotion all over her sensual body but figured from her demeanor that she would object to his overture. So, he waited and tried not looking over at her or at least make it obvious when he would. He couldn't help himself. He knew seeing her deep brown eyes would weaken him, the way that it had done so long ago when they spent their first evening together getting acquainted. That first evening years ago, Layla had shown tenderness towards him that he could not fully understand despite an outward sorrow that Daniel could sense. Perhaps, she held her own secrets. But when he was next to her, he always felt a sense of love and loyalty that he had never felt with any other woman. After the incident with Leon the preceding day, Daniel sensed that things had changed in his relationship with Layla and her feelings towards him. He feared how much they had changed.

An hour passed and then two. Walks along the beach together interrupted their relaxation on the chaise lounges. But still, no words were exchanged. The twinkle and flirtation in Layla's eyes were now extinguished like a fire once burning bright but now dead, not even the embers were burning. Even Layla wondered what happened. Had a new fire been replaced? One which itself had died out years ago, but which came back to life, slowly and perhaps inevitably. Did she will it so? Or was it the sacrifice that she witnessed? Or so it seemed.

Her mind spoke: "*Leon traveled all the way here to win me back? He must really love me? He never gave up on me. On us. I must have made a difference in him. No other woman loved him the way that I did. No other woman sacrificed for him the way that I did. No other woman moved cross country to be with him. He realizes that now. He realizes that he can never find another woman like me. He can never have a woman like me.*"

Those thoughts invigorated Layla. They instilled in her a sense of self-worth that she had not understood before. How could she let it go? After all the passage of time, there must be something between them. He crossed heaven and earth to be with her in this remote place in the Caribbean. She should give him a chance, give them a chance. Otherwise, she would regret it and feel like she settled. Was Daniel a consolation prize? She could have more. She would be more. She would be his First Lady and he, her King.

Layla hadn't realized that her secret thoughts had in actuality been conveyed to Daniel aloud. He lay there, listening to her in silence. She also voiced concerns about her safety with Daniel after she witnessed the injured Leon on the floor from Daniel's push. She no longer felt safe being with him in such a romantic and intimate place.

When Daniel asked if he should leave, Layla said "yes," never really looking at him or acknowledging his existence.

AFTER PACKING HIS LUGGAGE, Daniel walked to the front desk of the hotel. He asked the attendant if she could arrange a shuttle to the airport. She made the necessary arrangements on the phone. Within fifteen minutes, he was headed to the Luis Munoz Marin International Airport in San Juan.

DINNER

FAJARDO, PUERTO RICO

Later That Night

"Yᴇs, I'll have the lobster tail and she will have the halibut." Leon tucked a white napkin on his lap after first wiping his lips from eating the appetizer, calamari. Some guava aioli had stuck to the corner of his bottom lip after the last bite.

"Yes, sir." The waiter walked away to place the order.

Layla was happy that Leon took her to a nice seafood restaurant overlooking the Atlantic Ocean. She tried to forget that it was near the same location where the red and yellow kayaks launched to the luminescent bio bay earlier that week. Thoughts of Daniel danced in her head, but she forced them out. She was with her man now. Will Leon forgive her for being in Puerto Rico with another man? He must have already forgiven her if he wanted to be with her now.

"Thank you, babe. That sounds delicious." Layla was used to Leon ordering for her. When they first dated, she was against it. Layla was used to chivalry but somehow felt ordering for her was beyond expectations. After several conversations, Leon finally convinced Layla that, as the man and the head of the relationship, he should know what she liked and that she should accept that. Ultimately, she relented and felt comfortable with Leon picking her meals.

"You're welcome. I know that you also eat fish now." He glared at her across the table with an uncomfortable grin.

Layla was surprised. She wasn't a vegan or a pescatarian when she stopped dating Leon almost three years ago. They always ate burgers or steaks when they went out. After the breakup, Leon had called and texted her periodically, but she never told him that she became a pescatarian. Layla deleted Leon as a Facebook friend when she moved back to New York after she left her job in Tempe, Arizona. So, he could not have seen her various posts declaring the decision to no longer be strictly vegan. She wondered which one of her friends shared this with him. Was he spying on her or having her friends spy on her? Did he also know about her brief relationship with Roland earlier in the year? Leon must have because she posted once or twice about her dates with Roland. Whoever was spying on her for Leon surely told him about Roland. Layla didn't want to think of the implications. She just wanted to enjoy a lovely evening with Leon.

Sitting across from Leon, Layla had many questions that she wanted answered. Why did he come to Puerto Rico? How did he know that she was here? She wanted to tell him that she had never slept with Daniel but bringing up sex with the conservative Leon was out of the question. Besides, it was none of his business. She was sure that in the preceding years, Leon had been with other women. Several women in his congregation threw themselves at him when Layla was dating him. How could she blame them? Leon was well-spoken and handsome despite his short stature. She was certain that plenty of women were pleased when they learned that Leon was no longer with Layla. The promise of being First Lady was alluring and most women could not resist the temptation. Even Layla struggled with it. Was she struggling with it now? She did not know. And frankly, she did not care. She was happy to simply be with Leon.

"This is a wonderful evening," Leon added with a sense of accomplishment as he looked around the near-empty restaurant. He had only hoped that the Kasavista restaurant had a roaring fire to enhance the ambiance. He knew Layla was used to the extremely cold winters in New York and thought she would appreciate a reminder from home. Leon was unaware of the year-round warm temperatures of the Caribbean and how such necessities were not needed in Puerto Rico, even during the winters.

"Are you still in need of a First Lady?" Her boldness echoed in her voice such that she even surprised herself. She stared intently into his eyes, waiting for an answer, waiting for forgiveness.

"You will always be my First Lady, Lay. You're all that I ever wanted."

A lovely smile graced her lips.

Layla had professed her love for Leon years ago when they first dated. He had never voiced the same. This was the closest that Leon came to opening up and sharing his feelings for her. He was so guarded after the divorce. Layla feared that he could never give his heart to anyone again, not even to her. A part of her still hoped that he would tell her someday that he truly loved her. But tonight, this would suffice. It reassured her that she made the right choice, that she knew after a while that he would come to his senses and realize that she truly loved him despite all of their setbacks and trials. Her heart endured so much pain. Tonight, was her reward.

When the waiter brought out the signature soufflé for dessert, Layla was willing to try it despite the dairy ingredients. This pleased Leon. They shared a single dish together with Layla, at times, serving pieces of the soufflé to Leon using her fork.

Layla was startled when Leon's phone rang. He picked it up with his left hand and brought it to his ear. He recognized the female caller. Covering the microphone on the bottom of his cellphone with his right hand, Leon said, "Excuse me. I need to take this." He walked out to the patio to speak in private. Layla's eyes followed him anxiously, never letting him out of her sight. When he was far enough away so that Layla could not hear him, he felt comfortable enough to restart the conversation. "Ok, I can talk now."

"Hey, baby. I miss you," Okevia's gentle voice easily betrayed her excitement.

"I miss you too, babe." Leon held back the urge to blow a kiss like he normally did when speaking to Okevia over the phone. Surely, Layla would be suspicious if she saw him do that. He hoped that Okevia would not object and mention it during their conversation.

"When are you coming back?"

"In a bit. The church conference is still going on. Pastor Julio said that he may want me to preach at Sunday's service." Leon looked into the restaurant and saw Layla gazing at him. He shrugged his shoulders at her and smiled.

"I wish that I was there."

"You'll love Puerto Rico. It's beautiful."

"I can't wait. Maybe next year?"

"Sure, baby. Whatever you want. Sorry, it wasn't in the budget this year. Hey, gotta go."

Leon didn't wait for Okevia to respond. He ended the call and confidently walked inside, back to the table.

"Is everything alright?" Layla hesitantly asked.

"Yes. Just some problems at the church. I'm gone for a bit and everything goes to hell in a handbasket. What will they do without me?" Leon's devious grin was telling.

"Do you need to get back?"

"Nonsense. I'm here for you. For us."

He continued eating the soufflé nonchalantly while Layla wondered what was truly happening.

PALOMINITOS ISLAND

FAJARDO, PUERTO RICO

The Next Morning

THE DOOR to the funicular closed and it slowly descended the incline from the cliff at the top of the El Conquistador Resort and Spa to its private marina below. A second funicular was already at the marina and began its ascent. Lush tropical trees lined both sides of the two railways where the funiculars traversed. A small group of people was inside the descending funicular observing the views, including Palominos Island which was in the far distance. Layla and Leon embraced so as to steady themselves as the funicular descended. The incline slightly pulled them down towards the front of the funicular. Almost two-thirds of the way down, the funicular stopped, and an elderly couple exited so that they could enter their guest room in Las Olas Village, a secluded hotel wing etched into the side of the cliff. A few more guests also entered the funicular. Continuing its descent, the funicular arrived at its final destination. Everyone exited, including Layla and Leon. Some kids ran merrily towards Coqui

Water Park to enjoy their day. Their parents followed slowly behind them.

The breeze from the Caribbean swirled along the storefronts of the marina's shops. The bustling of workers readying the marina's cafe could barely be heard above the rapid flapping of the US and Puerto Rican flags atop the cafe's blue roof. A large white and blue trimaran was docked to the far left. Hotels guests embarked onto the trimaran to their voyage across the waters to the hotel's private island, Palominos Island.

Layla wondered what Leon had in store for them on this bright, sunny morning.

"The fresh air is wonderful," she exclaimed.

"Yes, it is." Leon paused for a moment. "I hope you don't get seasick."

"I... I really don't know to be honest with you." She was perplexed.

Leon walked towards a Sea Ray yacht docked at the rear of the marina. Layla followed. It was a forty-foot 470 Sundancer. As they approached, a steward greeted them aboard on the full beam swim platform just behind the transom. When they were comfortable, the steward showed them to the sunroom behind the cockpit. As she was walking in the sunroom, Layla slipped on the cherry wood floor and almost lost her balance. But Leon caught her, breaking her fall.

"You ok?" Leon asked.

Layla nodded. She was a little embarrassed having never been on a yacht before.

They both sat down on a plush sofa in the sunroom and looked out the windows towards the turquoise waters beyond.

Captain Esteban was at the helm staring at two widescreen displays. He pushed a few buttons and worked the joystick to his right. As the yacht went underway, the roar of the double diesel engines filled the air. The ride was comfortable even when the captain increased the throttle to full power. The yacht, however, was only traveling about 17 knots for most of the brief trip. The boat exhibited good wave penetration, throwing water low and wide as it fared the ocean. Layla was amazed at how pleasant the ride was. She wondered why Leon even inquired about seasickness.

After the trip began, Leon decided that the couple should sit on the foredeck to fully appreciate the spectacular views as they headed towards Palominitos Island, a small cay about four miles east of Fajardo and just off the coast of the larger Palominos Island. They walked to the bow barely holding onto the cabin side grab-rails to steady themselves because the ride was so smooth. The protective side rails and stanchions also ensured that they did not fall into the water while walking to the bow.

While the boat accelerated at times, there was minimal bow rise. This did not interrupt the couple's enjoyment of the views while they relaxed on the foredeck.

When they finally arrived at Palominitos Island, the hydraulic swim platform was lowered by a member of the crew. Leon and Layla walked to the stern and then down the platform. They briefly waded calves-deep into the warm Caribbean waters. They then walked onto the white sand beach of the narrow cay, which had a handful of palm trees and other vegetation. Waiting for them was a red blanket, a basket full of fruit with other snacks, and a chilled bottle of champagne.

Layla strolled the sandy cay. The sand was so white it looked more like sugar. She kicked the sand at spots to determine if this paradise was truly real and not a dream or a figment of her imagination. Her smile brightened.

When she walked back to the red blanket and food spread, Leon asked, "You thirsty?" He handed her a glass of champagne and took a sip out of his own glass. He scanned the horizon taking in the tropical views. The salty air was refreshing.

"Thank you, babe." Layla searched for words to express her gratitude.

She was amazed at how things had changed drastically between them. When she moved to Tempe, Arizona three years ago, she often noticed that Leon was very frugal and rarely spent money on her. She was the one who mainly paid when they went to dinner or a movie, mostly because Leon's church finances were struggling. She convinced several of her coworkers to attend Leon's church. Originally, he was against it, but he relented when Layla expressed that their tithes could help with the church's situation. She never realized that Leon would be doing so well after her efforts.

Now he was lavishing her with luxury. He was treating her like his First Lady; the way that he promised so long ago - the way that she so deserved. She only hoped that he would treat her the same way in public when they were with his congregation or with his family.

After finishing the champagne in his glass, Leon sat down on the blanket with his legs crossed. He gestured towards her to sit next to him. Layla did and laid her head across his chest. The two were like lovebirds starting all over again in this tropical oasis. Nothing could separate them. Not the distance between their two States. Not their family and friends. Not their past with all its faults. It was as if time stood still on this remote island at the edge of the Caribbean.

At that moment, Layla never wanted to leave this place. She never wanted to face the realities of her new job or her family. If Leon could always hold her the way that he was now, then she would be content. She would feel the love that she desperately needed after feeling rejected by her past relationships. Could Leon's heart also rejoice the way hers was now? She only hoped that it would.

She turned her head towards Leon's face. His eyes seemed hollow as if he was deep in contemplation as he looked endlessly towards the rhythmic ocean. When her eyes met his eyes, he snapped out of it and held her tighter. That comforted her. She sensed Leon did not want to lose her again. She wondered how much he was hurting after she left him. Their relationship was at a standstill all this time. Would they have been engaged by now or perhaps even married? It would not matter anymore. She vowed to do everything she could to make up for lost time.

MARINA

FAJARDO, PUERTO RICO

Later That Afternoon

AFTER THE SUNDANCER docked again several hours later at the El Conquistador Resort and Spa's private marina where it was originally docked that morning, Layla and Leon disembarked. They thanked the crew for a lovely and memorable trip. Finding their bodies drained from the glowing sun and slightly tipsy, the couple slowly walked from the slip where the boat was docked in the rear of the marina back to the area by the shops nearest to the funicular. A few people were huddled at the cafe eating a late lunch. The roar of the trimaran's engines could be heard as it approached full of guests returning from Palominos Island.

Walking arm in arm, Layla smiled, holding back a gleefulness that she hadn't experienced in a while. She looked at Leon who seemed pensive. A part of her wanted to ask what was on his mind, but she thought that he would tell her at the appropriate time. So, she didn't bother to ask.

"I had a wonderful time," she said, hoping to garner his attention away from his thoughts. "It was lovely. The island is so quaint."

Leon turned his head toward Layla, acknowledging her comment. "Yes, it is. No one is going to believe that we spent the day on a private island in Puerto Rico." Leon grinned until he realized that he told his congregation that he was at a church conference in San Juan. "*Surely they won't mind if I took some time to relax and enjoy the island,*" he thought. "*I deserve it. I haven't been on a vacation in years.*"

His concern turned to Layla. Leon only hoped that she would not post anything on Facebook about meeting him in Puerto Rico and their trip to Palominitos Island. Otherwise, members of his congregation who were still friends with Layla would find out and tell the others that Leon had lied to them and went on an escapade to win Layla back at the congregation's expense. "*She'll keep quiet. She knows better. I've drilled it into her a long time ago that our relationship is private and no one's business.*" That thought brought Leon a quiet comfort, but he worried that the intervening years since they broke up may have loosened his grip on her.

"We should head back and freshen up," Leon said as he now looked away and relinquished Layla's arm. His face betrayed his underlying concerns and he did not want Layla to discover it.

"That's a great idea." Layla wondered what was in store. She hoped that they could relax at their respective hotel rooms before the evening's festivities.

The two continued walking. Before reaching the funicular, Leon's phone vibrated. He grabbed his phone and noticed that he just received a text from Okevia: "Hope you're enjoying your day, hun." The text was a surprise but brought a smile to his face. He motioned towards Layla and said, "I need to find a restroom. I'll be right back."

He scurried away like a jack-rabbit trying to escape a predator.

Before long, he was out of sight, leaving Layla puzzled and confused. She scoured the marina for a place to sit down. Other than

La Marina Cafe, there were no other outside seating areas. So, she walked back to the cafe. She sat down on a bar stool and placed her bag on her lap. Checking her iPhone, she noticed that she had missed two calls while on the island: one from her youngest daughter, Amirah, and one from Roland Lark. Roland left a voicemail message. Nervously, she pushed the play button and raised the phone to her head:

Hey Lay, it's me, Roland. Hopefully, you haven't forgotten my voice. Anyway, I'm... I've been thinking about you ever since I bumped into you at work. It was good seeing you again. You looked great. I know you're on vacation and I probably shouldn't be bothering you. But I hope we can talk about... about us. So, when you get this message, give me a call...

The voicemail message ended as if the phone call was interrupted or the caller ended the call abruptly for no apparent reason; at least not a reason discernible by the listener. Layla wondered why Roland called her now of all times. She had not heard from him in months until she saw him at the airport earlier in the week. He had long since escaped her mind once she started seeing Daniel. Now that she was finally back with Leon, this complicated the situation even further. Layla wondered should she call Roland back.

She looked around but Leon was nowhere to be found.

"*I should tell him not to call me anymore,*" she agreed to herself and then pushed the "call back" icon on her iPhone.

"Hello." Roland's strong voice comforted Layla even now for some unknown reason. "Hey, Lay," he added after realizing who was calling him.

The sounds of Roland walking faster echoed through to Layla's phone. He sought a quiet place away from the bustling noise of the concourse. Although he was still at work, Layla's call was very important to him. "Thanks for calling me back. I wasn't sure if you would. How are you doing? How's Puerto Rico?"

Roland wasn't sure if he should bring up a vacation with another man. But he wanted Layla to know that he still cared about her even if his approach was somewhat awkward. He hoped to overcome it somehow.

"It's beautiful here, but that's not why I am calling." Roland could hear the exasperation in her voice.

"Okay?" He waited for the inevitable.

"I need you to stop."

"Stop what? Stop loving you? Stop caring about you? Stop wanting you back in my life? I don't want to stop. Lay, you are the best thing that happened to me. I didn't realize that then, but I do now. I'm sorry for hurting you."

Upon hearing these words, Layla sighed deeply and felt a sense of relief.

"Thank you, Roland. You don't know how much that means to me."

"I know that I don't deserve a second chance, but I want a second chance. I need one."

"Roland..."

Layla felt her iPhone being forcefully dislodged from her hand. She tried to grip it tighter as she wondered what was happening. As she turned her head, she saw Leon standing beside her.

"Who the fuck is Roland?" Leon barked with his typical loud, angry voice which resounded throughout the marina for all to hear. He spoke into the phone, "Lose this phone number, loser."

Leon angrily threw Layla's iPhone onto the concrete ground with such tremendous force, smashing it.

"I'm gone for a minute and this is what you do? You call another man! I can't believe this."

"Leon, it's not what you think..."

ROLAND

ELMHURST, NEW YORK

Later That Night

THE MOONLIGHT SHONE partially into the sleeping area of the small studio apartment, barely illuminating the part of the room nearest the window facing the busy street. Seated in the nearly darkened room was Roland, dejected and confused. He had been sitting there alone for hours after he returned home from work. After that afternoon's unplanned call to Layla, he wondered what to do next. Desperation filled his entire body and angered him even more. With clenched fists, Roland pounded the nightstand next to him such that it shook violently, causing the lamp to fall to the floor. He gave no heed to the shattered lamp or anything else. All he could focus on was Layla.

"How could this be happening?" he thought. *"I'm not gonna let her go."*

He paced the diminutive room vigorously despite not being able to see clearly in the dark. Searching the depths of his mind for an answer, he could not find one. It only made his despair worsen and quickened his beating heart.

Roland looked around for something, anything, to guide him. But he knew that this was not a local issue where he could walk to a neighborhood block to confront a bully. In the past, because of his size, Roland often used his physical prowess to make people conform to his will. No, this was something beyond his control. His imagination spun like a whirlwind out of control. Layla was thousands of miles away in the Caribbean. And with him! Roland realized that Layla was not vacationing with Daniel as she had told him earlier in the week when they meet at the airport. But him; the monster who had destroyed her life, who had bruised and battered her soul so often.

After what he had been told about Leon, disbelief overcame Roland. Leon interfered with Roland's past relationship with Layla with overt threats of violence. Threats not only to Roland, but also to Layla.

After the abrupt call, Roland wondered what happened. What should he do? What could he do? And then it came to him. "*I need... I need someone to calm me down... to give me what I am lacking.*" The thought emboldened him in a senseless way that he could not understand. Roland grabbed his cellphone and frantically looked for Darren's number.

"You know it's a Sunday night. You should be getting ready for bed," Darren's voice bellowed through the phone before Roland could even speak. Even the loud music in the background did not drown out his heavy, authoritarian voice.

"Where are you?" Roland asked surprisingly. But he knew that Darren frequented a local bar near his apartment in Hell's Kitchen. Tonight would be no different.

"It doesn't matter. Tell momma what's on your mind."

The disco music slowly faded as Darren walked out of the bar and onto the busy street. Passersby stared but he took no heed of them and continued walking until he reached the street corner.

"It's Layla," Roland sheepishly answered.

Unexpectedly, Darren's eyes rolled. Luckily, Roland couldn't see or sense his exasperation. He stayed calm for Roland's sake. "What happened?"

"She's with Leon. In Puerto Rico."

"What? You're kidding me."

"No. I called her and he answered the phone."

"Are you sure?"

"We went to high school together. I know his creepy voice anywhere."

"What are you going to do?" Darren already expected the typical macho response, but he had to hear it from Roland himself before answering.

"He threatened me. I can't believe that asshole threatened me. I'm worried about Layla and what he will do to her. I told you how he is." His mind raced as Roland remembered the call abruptly ending when the phone smashed into pieces onto the ground. "I need to be there for her. She needs me now more than ever."

"There's no way you can get to Puerto Rico tonight. It's late. The earliest that you can get there is tomorrow afternoon."

"I know. I know. I waited too long. I should have left when I found out this afternoon. What was I thinking?" Roland wanted to add how helpless he felt, but he knew that Darren already sensed it.

"She may not even be there when your plane arrives. Do you even know what part of the island she is staying?"

Roland reluctantly admitted that he did not know about Layla's travel plans. He didn't even know if she was actually in Puerto Rico. She may be in Arizona visiting Leon for all he knew. His heart sank even further, but that was an unconscious and unexpected sense of relief. He realized that a trip to Puerto Rico would be senseless, unfruitful, and a waste of his time. What would Flor think? She would certainly find out that he spent their hard-earned money traipsing around the world for some other woman. That would mean the end of their fragile relationship. Roland wasn't sure if he was willing to give up his relationship with Flor anymore now that he learned that Layla was with Leon.

"Look, momma gets it. You waited thirty-two years to ask Layla out. And for a few months she was secretly yours. She's your dream woman from your childhood. But it's just a fantasy. You need to think about yourself and your future. Do you even have a future with Layla?"

Roland began to take deeper breaths as he listened to Darren's voice. His mind raced to various recent memories with Layla: their trip to Staten Island, the night at the top of the Empire State building with 360-degree views of the city and watching ice skaters at Lincoln Center. A few more memories graced his mind.

"It's just that we are so good together."

"Oh really? Is that why she is not with one but two men in Puerto Rico? Don't kid yourself, Roland. You deserve better."

"She's the best that I've ever had," Roland secretly frowned as reality surfaced to the fore.

"Are you sure? I don't think you believe that. If you did, then you would have left Flor months ago like I told you."

The sting struck deep and true.

Roland wanted to lash out, but he knew that would make him a hypocrite.

"Where's Flor now?" Darren switched the topic as a way to ease the tension and calm Roland down. He knew that Roland truly loved Flor even though Roland didn't recognize it himself. Speaking of Flor always brought Roland to his senses.

"She's with her family in Stamford."

Roland realized that she had not called nor texted all day. Neither had he.

"You're all by yourself. And lonely. Don't kid yourself. Do you want to come meet me at the club? Stan and the rest of the guys are here. They would love to see you again. You haven't been by since you started at Liberty."

Hesitating, Roland agreed.

A DISTANT HOPE

RIO GRANDE, PUERTO RICO

The Next Day

When Layla realized that her mind was so deep in thought that she missed a phone call on the hotel's hospitality phone, she was both disheartened and relieved. Her body was still shaking from the anxiety of dealing with Leon the previous day. She had a wonderful experience boating to Palominitos Island, only to find that Leon's controlling and overbearing jealousy destroyed another memory that should have been blissful and enduring. Her tattered iPhone was on the end table next to the hotel bed, indicative of the current state of their relationship. Despite her efforts to steady herself, the long sleepless night left her body weary and in need of encouragement. She decided to seek encouraging words from the only person that loved her unconditionally and who understood her in ways that she could not fully comprehend. So, she made the long-distance call to California, unaware of the four-hour difference.

The voice on the other end was initially hesitant until Layla reluctantly spoke, easily betraying an inner sense of nervousness.

"Dad, it's me, Layla." She held back tears. She was his oldest child and despite the small age difference between them, her father adored her and looked up to Layla because she was his most successful child. In some ways, she dreaded shattering his image of her.

"Baby girl, what's wrong?" His authoritative voice echoed his past experience as a teacher at a school district in a minority neighborhood not too far from where he grew up. His students teased that he learned how to be a strict disciplinarian after serving in the Air Force. But he denied that vehemently. Now that he was retired from teaching, he continued using this voice but only with his eight, adult children.

"I don't know." Layla seemed genuinely confused.

"Yes, you do. You wouldn't have called me if you didn't. I've taught all of my kids to be humble but honest. You know that, Lay."

She surely did. It was ingrained into her since she was a child and was one of her earliest memories of her father. Honesty, however, was something that she struggled with at that moment. Her father never liked Leon even though he was not aware of the emotional abuse let alone the physical abuse. Layla feared disclosing it now. Her father waited patiently until Layla mustered the strength to tell him what was on her mind.

"I just need to hear your voice," she said in a child-like manner.

"Okay. Okay. Well, Cissy and I are going to the Poppy Festival later today. I've designed several new T-shirts for the festival including a tribute to Aretha Franklin. It's marvelous. Eddie drew it. I think you will like it."

"That's awesome. Eddie's drawings look very realistic." Her cheerfulness resurfaced. "Are you going to send me pictures?"

"Of course, as usual." His bountiful smile mirrored Layla's smile. They were often teased as being twins rather than father and daughter. His words brought that smile to Layla's mind, even though she could not see it. She regretted not being able to FaceTime her father, but this would do for now.

"I would like that."

"... David, honey, we need to leave." A female voice could be heard in the distance along with some rumbling of boxes.

"Just a minute. I'll be right there." He tried to cover the speaker, but Layla could still hear the voice of her father's newest wife.

"I'll let you go, Dad. Thanks for being there for me. Love you."

"Love you too, baby girl." He paused and took a deep breath. "Just remember that all things work out for the good of those who love God and who are called according to His purpose. Whatever it is, it will work out. If not, I still have my Glock." He laughed heartily and Layla unconsciously joined in.

"Thanks, Dad."

She hung up the hospitality phone with full assurance.

◊ ◊ ◊

AFTER TAKING A LONG, welcome shower, Layla hastily dressed. She put on a white bathing suit similar to the one that she wore earlier in the week when Daniel was her companion at the Wyndham Grand Rio Mar. She put her long, black velvet hair into a ponytail and placed her beach hat on. A deep purple swimsuit wrap hung on her waist. She slipped on a pair of T-strip sandals and walked to the public beach adjacent to the resort. The beach crowd was minimal, which was a welcome surprise.

Seated on a bronze, chaise lounge, Layla gazed into the endless aqua blue of the Atlantic. The breeze engulfed her body as if it was cleansing her soul and releasing any impurities heavenward. With the breeze were also her thoughts swirling around; gentle and betrayed. Surprisingly, her first thought was of Daniel and how she told him in a spot not too far from where she was resting that she felt unsafe. Was that a mistake? At that moment, she felt it was. He never made her feel unsafe. Daniel made her feel loved and welcomed. He not only lavished her with praise because of her outward beauty, but he also praised her mind, her gentleness and happiness that he envied despite the hardships of her youth.

Why did Leon follow her here? Was he trying to destroy what she had with Daniel out of envy and spite? Layla grimaced at the thought. She had finally opened up and would have let love into her life again if not for an overreaction. She was unwilling to forgive when he needed it so. Now, she had lost Daniel's love and she realized it. He was back in the States by now, back at his law firm busying himself. Layla knew that Daniel wouldn't forget her, but he would leave her alone and respect her decision even if she now regretted it herself. Layla knew that in the preceding years while he was waiting for her, Daniel dated other women, but none captured him like Layla. She wondered if he would date again but realized that his heart needed time to heal just like hers did. She never knew Daniel to be a player like Leon with his many women. A part of her held out hope that someday they may see each other again and rekindle a relationship even if it was a distant hope.

Without warning, Layla's mind focused on Roland. Why was he so persistent after avoiding her for so long? Why would he call her when he knew that she was vacationing in Puerto Rico with another man? Was he trying to sabotage her relationship as well? That thought angered her in a way that she did not fully understand. Yet, she was subconsciously flattered at his overtures. Would he forgive her for the spectacle that he had to endure? Layla knew that Roland was overprotective and his previous comments berating Leon and threatening him scared her. She was glad that Roland wanted to come to her rescue but wondered whether he suffered from the same control issues as Leon.

Three men, a trifecta of sorts, confused her and took her out of herself. She was apprehensive about it. Just then, unexpectedly, a pure blue butterfly sailed delicately through the air and landed on her right hand. Its bright, colorful wings fluttered twice, revealing its

full majesty. Layla stood still in hopes of not startling the blue butterfly. As she did so, Layla calmed down from the excitement and
anxiety that briefly overcame her while thinking of the men in her
life. Sensing her response, the butterfly turned towards her as if to
match her eyes and then it glided away as quickly as it appeared. A
deep breath of Caribbean air refreshed Layla's thoughts. An inner
brightness showed her the way. She knew that her last day in Puerto
Rico would be fine and the future hopeful. Avoiding Leon and traveling home alone, though not ideal, was the right thing to do.

AN EMPTY FRIDGE

MIDDLETOWN, NEW YEAR

A Month Later

WHEN LAYLA OPENED the door to the stainless steel refrigerator door in her kitchen, the internal light shone so brightly in her eyes that the glare nearly woke her half-awake self. The bottles of various condiments; pickles, pepperoncini, mustard, mayonnaise, *sofrito*, soy sauce, among others, clanked loudly as the door nearly extended fully open. Layla had to quickly stop it from slamming against the wall. Bottles of lemonade and orange juice were on the top shelf. A day-old salad from the hospital cafeteria was on another shelf. Most of the other refrigerator shelves were empty. Layla contemplated going to the grocery store to meal prep and stock her refrigerator, but she changed her mind.

"*I'm a single bachelorette,*" she thought. "*Between my work hours and the long commute, my work week is over fifty hours. I don't have time to cook.*" That thought gave her some relief until Layla realized that her daughter, Amirah, would be visiting her later that evening after Amira got off of work.

Layla remembered that Amirah would often drop by unexpectedly and berate her mother for not having any food to eat. She always wanted her mother to cook for her when she visited. Amirah's favorite dish was Jamaican Jerk Chicken. She always wanted some *Jollof* rice to accompany the meal. Layla knew that the meal wouldn't take that long for her to prepare. She had made jerk chicken for Amirah and her other children many times before. Exhausted, Layla reassured herself that she was done cooking for her children. She cooked five to six meals a week for over twenty years and now was her own time to relax and care for herself. If she felt like eating out every day, who had the right to complain? If she wanted food delivered by Uber Eats, then she could do so even if the food was not healthy or it did not fit into her pescatarian lifestyle. Sure, her body may suffer for the day or two. But she had all the free time to exercise at the gym to work it off for however long she wanted. Layla no longer felt like she had to hurry home to cater to one of her children's needs. They were all adults now and out of the house. Layla was the classical empty nester.

Determined to shut down her daughter before she called out Layla for not cooking again, Layla decided to text her daughter and give her a head's up:

"I was gonna cook. I changed my mind and resigning out of protest! You hungry... Eat before you come! Bloop"

Layla smiled out of her new sense of liberation. She knew that her daughter would understand now that Amirah was busy herself with her corporate marketing job that frequently required traveling throughout the country. Amirah moved from the small town of Middletown to the big city to follow her career and to be closer to her boyfriend. A year had passed since she moved out, but Amirah still visited her mother once or twice a month when she could.

"It's okay, Mom. I'll pick up some food from Cosimos and bring some over."

Layla was pleased with Amirah's response and her new-found independence. "*I raised her right.*" Layla comforted herself with that thought. Her children deserved the world that Layla did not have growing up: family, friends, education, travels to foreign lands, financial independence. The only thing that Layla regretted was not modeling the marital love that she wanted her children to experience with their future spouse. Two failed marriages and the brutal relationship with Leon haunted her.

When she started dating Roland earlier that year, Layla thought it would all change. She could redeem herself in her children's eyes because Roland was more attentive and enamored by her, unlike Leon. Roland Lark also attended the same high school as Layla. He was a football player when she was the cheerleading captain of the Lynwood High School cheerleading squad. Oftentimes during the game, she would see Roland staring at her when he should have been paying attention to the quarterback announcing the next play during the huddle. The other team members noticed that their tight end rarely followed the plays. Lucky for them, the rest of the team made up for his inattentiveness. But that didn't stop Roland from outperforming the others. He desperately wanted to impress Layla by his athletic prowess, but he was too shy to ask her out. Everyone else said it was because Roland was afraid of Papa Little. All the boys were and rightfully so.

But by the end of the first semester of her junior year, Roland finally mustered the courage to ask Layla to the homecoming dance. He was one year older than her and eligible to run for the homecoming court. When she quietly accepted the invitation, Roland was ecstatic. He spent the entire week planning what he was going to wear. He even practiced his dances moves with his younger sister, Gwen. When Roland forgot the corsage, Gwen had one for him. The night with Roland was magical. They danced all night and never left each other's side. Roland even snuck a goodnight kiss on the porch without Papa Little noticing. After that night, the young couple continued to date until graduation. Roland moved away to attend Oklahoma University on a football scholarship.

The distance ended the relationship. By then, Layla attended Manuel Dominguez High School for her senior year. The new environment made it easier to forget a young love. It is also where she met her oldest daughter's father. She moved to New York in her early twenties shortly after she was married and was pregnant with Jasmine. Layla never saw Roland again until he moved to New York. And then it was only happenstance.

Although they only went out on a couple of dates when they finally met up again, their telephone conversations were always fun, heartfelt, and secretly exhilarating. Layla was giddy again and that was welcome. She had plans on seeing Roland again until he seemed to rebuff every overture that she made with excuses that even a teenager would think were lame. Layla wondered if it was her. Was it her three children? Her two divorces? Her night job? Her eagerness? She did not understand why Roland kept his distance after the last date. When he stopped answering her calls and returning her texts, she suspected that he liked another woman. She was not aware that he was living with Flor the whole time.

The chance meeting at Newark Liberty Airport was surprising. Layla's feelings for Roland resurfaced somewhat once he called her in Puerto Rico. The strong and confident Roland came to mind; the one that protected her in her youth. But where was it going? She did not know.

OTHER PROSPECTS

GILBERT, ARIZONA

Around the Same Time

DANIEL MENDOZA ARRIVED HOME EARLY after spending most of the day in a mediation in downtown Phoenix. The hour-long drive home was exhausting. Daniel was hungry, having not eaten anything for lunch. The mediator believed that empty stomachs made the parties eager to settle. However, that wasn't the case. Empty stomachs made people irritable and ornery and, in Daniel's experience, unlikely to compromise and resolve the litigation. That's exactly what happened. With no resolution, the parties now had to move forward with the trial and prepare for the consequences of having a jury decide their fate.

Trying to get the day's activities behind him, Daniel decided to cook a quick meal in his Tovala oven. Prepping the chef-assembled meal took about a minute. The smart oven was activated by an app on Daniel's iPhone after he placed the two tins of sweet ginger roasted salmon and vegetable rice inside. It took approximately thirteen minutes for the Tovala to cycle through the various steam, bake, and broil cycles before the meal was perfectly cooked. Daniel knew that he would receive a notification on his Apple Watch that the process was complete. In the meantime, he could walk away, undress, and text his niece, Marie.

"Hey, Marie. Just checking on you. Hope you're doing well." Daniel's iPhone originally indicated that the text was delivered. Moments later, it indicated that the text was read by the recipient. When no response was immediately forthcoming, Daniel continued undressing in his master bedroom. Daniel untied his tie and then removed his cuff links

"Alexa, connect iPhone." The Amazon echo's circular edge glowed a tint of sapphire blue alternating with a lighter turquoise blue. In the background, he heard, "Searching... now connected to Daniel's iPhone."

"Alexa, play Lovely Bones."

The symphonic sounds of a piano filled the room, echoing throughout the house. Then the soft, yet sultry voice of a female singer, Tahirah Memory, quietly instilled the music with divine passion: "You don't ever get over it..." Daniel sighed deeply as the song played. In some ways, the lyrics mirrored his own anguish. He tried desperately to forget what transpired with Layla in Puerto Rico. It seemed so long ago. Could things have been different if he restrained his emotions? Would they still be together? Daniel shook those thoughts away like he did every night. But they kept coming back.

Daniel reached for his iPhone to make a call but decided against it. He had not spoken to Layla since he took the shuttle to the airport in San Juan, Puerto Rico. Uncertain of whether she even wanted to talk to him, Daniel continually resisted the temptation for what it seemed every night. He kept reminding himself that Layla felt unsafe around him. He didn't fully understand why she felt that way. Staying away from her was a way of respecting her decision.

Instead of calling Layla, when the Tovala notification went off,

Daniel plated his food and began eating in the family room alone. The Black List played on the television with pontifications from Raymond Reddington brightening Daniel's face with a smile. While enjoying the show, he received a call from Marie.

"Hey, Uncle Danny. What are you doing?"

"Nothing. Just watching TV."

"Alone again. You need to date. Stop staying at home. It's pathetic."

"I've tried that. It's hard to find a good woman my age. All of them are taken already."

"Uncle Danny, you know I love you and want the best for you. It makes me sad that you're alone. You should have a wife and kids."

"I'm too old for that."

"No, you're not. You can have kids at any age."

"Women my age already have kids. Some have grandkids."

"Well, you need to date someone younger. Someone in their twenties. You are a handsome guy and an attorney. Women will want you."

Daniel held back a smile but glumly said, "I want a woman who wants to grow old with me."

"Young women will."

"That's not been my experience or any of my friends who have dated younger women."

"Look, Uncle Danny. You need to get over that girl, whatever her name is."

"Layla."

"Whatever. I have a perfect girl for you."

Marie fiddled with her phone until she found a picture of her friend, Rochelle. When she found a flattering picture that she thought was enticing, Marie texted it to her uncle.

"I sent you a picture. Let me know when you receive it."

"Ok." Daniel waited patiently through the awkward silence. "Wow. She is very beautiful, but she's so young."

"She's twenty-eight actually. She likes older men."

"I don't know Marie. I usually date women who are no more than two or three years younger than me. Layla was an exception. She was five years younger than me and look how that turned out."

"Rochelle is very mature for her age. She also doesn't have any kids and wants kids someday."

Daniel looked at the picture again. Rochelle was undeniably attractive with an air of sophistication yet reserved. She was the type of woman Daniel would pursue if she was older.

"It's more of a generational difference," Daniel explained. "She probably doesn't like the same things that I like: music, movies, stuff like that. I don't drink or go clubbing. She's at the age where she still wants to do those things."

"You both just like the same stuff. She's like me: a homebody. She loves watching a lot of TV. She's very intelligent for her age. She's smarter than me." Marie laughed, hoping to lighten the mood.

"Women think I am pompous because I went to law school."

"She has a bachelors in health care administration and an associates in business. I don't think that she will feel that way."

"It doesn't matter to me if she has degrees. I've dated women who only graduated from high school. It just depends if they treat me right and are committed to the relationship. That's more important to me."

Daniel started feeling frustrated and uncomfortable with the conversation. Opening up to his niece about his interests in women and what he desired from relationships was something that he had never done before and did not want to do now.

"Marie, there's a big generational gap. As a beautiful woman, I'm sure that she can find a nice man her own age."

"Ok. I get it but she doesn't like men her own age. She dates older men. Even older than you."

"That's sad." Daniel's voice was telling.

Marie texted Rochelle what her uncle said in response to her inquiry. When Marie received a response from Rochelle, she continued the conversation with her uncle, "But ok. Rochelle said if you ever decide to stop judging her by her age to give her a call."

"I'll think about it."

Marie knew that her uncle would not give it a second thought. He was old-fashioned when it came to relationships, but she wanted to try to convince him otherwise. It was the least that she could do for him under the circumstances.

"I love you, Uncle Danny."

"Love you too."

When the call ended, Daniel thought about calling Layla again. He convinced himself not to.

HAMILTON

NEW YORK CITY, NEW YORK

Two Months Later

WHEN LAYLA WALKED OUTSIDE of the historic Rodgers Theatre, she asked Jeannie if she wanted to see Times Square. A Hamilton playbill was in her hand and the tune, "The Election of 1800," was inescapably on her mind. She wondered if American history would be different if Alexander Hamilton was on the presidential ticket. But such silly thoughts seemed inappropriate when the whole purpose of having Jeannie fly out from Dallas, Texas was to discuss "her predicament." At least, that is how Jeannie described it. It was an emergency of sorts and Jeannie dropped everything to be by her friend's side, even if it meant paying twice as much for airfare than the normal price. Nothing would keep her from being with Layla at this critical juncture in her life.

"That would be nice. I've never been to Times Square." Jeannie's full lips brightened into a smile.

Layla was no longer impressed by Times Square, having lived in

New York for more than two decades. She came only when friends visited from out of state. In recent years, that was few and far between. But because Layla had not seen Jeannie Thomas since they both attended Lynwood High School as teenagers, the tourist trap was a welcome distraction.

"Here, follow me."

The two walked up 46th Street towards Times Square. The night air was a little chilly. They walked the short distance arm in arm. Layla was still merry from the night's festivities, but Jeannie still sensed that her mind was pre-occupied.

"So, you've been avoiding the topic since you picked me up from La Guardia this morning. I know you wanted to talk about it. Why else would you ask me to come to visit you?"

Layla's recollection of the conversation was that Jeannie insisted, but she did not want to argue with an old friend, especially because she really needed her advice.

"I know. I'm embarrassed to say the least."

A group of six boys who looked in their late teens or early twenties was gathering a crowd for a hip-hop street dance performance. As more individuals stopped to watch the upcoming performance, Layla and Jeannie also paused. This gave the two friends a better opportunity to talk because they were no longer focused on weaving in and out of the pedestrian traffic.

"Has Leon called you again?"

Layla looked away from the street performers and gazed seriously towards Jeannie.

"Yeah, but I didn't answer this time."

"I'm proud of you for being strong."

"Girl, he's working hard to get me back. He sent me a picture of his manhood."

"What? You serious?"

"Yes, this isn't the first time."

"Isn't he a pastor?"

"Lord, please forgive me. Yes, he is. He doesn't always act like it." Layla was embarrassed to admit this.

"Does he think that a dick pic will win you back?"

"He thinks the sex was so great and because I've been alone for nearly a year without sex that I will be crawling back begging for more."

"Oh, my goodness. He's something." Jeannie's mouth opened wide, but she quickly closed it. Her bulging eyes, however, were not as easily concealed.

"You should have heard his reaction when I told him that the sex was not great and that I had better."

Jeannie's body shook uncontrollably as she tried to restrain herself. She accidentally dropped her playbill when she fanned the front of her mouth as a gesture of excitement. A tourist also waiting for the dance performance and secretly overhearing the conversation bent down to pick up the playbill and handed it to her.

"Thank you, kind sir," Jeannie politely said as she took the playbill from his hand. She refused to look him in the eyes out of a sense of embarrassment. Quickly trying not to let Layla escape from the conversation, Jeannie nudged her.

"I'm not going to say it here. I'll wait until we get home." Layla quietly but sternly responded to the nudge to her waist.

It was nearing midnight and Jeannie knew that it would be several hours before they would arrive back at Layla's house in upstate New York.

"So, what are you gonna do little lady," Jeannie persisted because she knew that was the real reason for her venture to New York.

Layla took a deep breath. "We've dated for five years. That's a long time. It was hard for me to give that up."

"Don't take offense. But you know how I feel. You deserve better."

"I know, Jeannie. I do deserve better than Leon." Her sigh was an obvious indicator of her eventual acknowledgment of the inevitable.

"Why haven't you been dating? What about that one guy who

lives here in New York who is also a knight? Roland? You were smitten with him in high school."

Jeannie's comments made Layla smile but with some anguish.

"I haven't heard from him since he called me when I was in Puerto Rico."

"He probably thinks you are back with Leon."

"I thought the same thing." Layla frowned as she spoke those words.

"You should give Roland a chance. He obviously likes you. Plus, he's here. You could be with him right now instead of your old crotchety girlfriend." Jeannie laughed half-heartedly in hopes of encouraging her friend, but she quickly subsided because she wanted to be mindful of Layla's mixed emotions.

"I think that shipped has sailed."

"Don't give up so easily. You reunited with him once after all these years. You can do it again. Its fate that you guys be together. Trust me."

Layla was unsure if Jeannie was being honest with her or if she was just trying to push Layla away from Leon. Jeannie never liked Leon especially after Layla told her about some of the eccentric things that he did or said. Layla never mentioned any of the physical abuse. But even Layla's children never liked Leon. Layla convinced herself that it was because no one saw what she saw in Leon: his vulnerability alongside his confidence. Jeannie couldn't understand. No one could.

"I won't write Roland off. I promise."

"Well, who else do you have in your life?" Jeannie was curious as to how Layla would answer this question.

"To be honest, no one. But Amirah wants me to reconnect with Daniel. She said that I was the happiest with him. The happiest that she has seen me in years."

"Have you heard from him?"

"No, not really."

"Not even a text message?"

Layla felt even more dejected.

"No. No texts or calls."

"Have you tried calling him?"

"We haven't spoken since he took the shuttle to the airport in San Juan. I haven't called."

"There has to be a reason why."

As Jeannie made that last remark, the male performers began to dance. The crowd gathered closer. Cheers and claps echoed in the night air. Layla's focus turned to the performers and their young and vibrant physique. Jeannie inevitably focused on them as well. She knew that this opportunity was lost for now, but she had a sense of accomplishment that their conversation was productive. Maybe Layla questioned getting back with Leon. Jeannie's uncertainty only fueled her commitment to protecting her friend.

"Ladies and Gentlemen. Give it up for Rashid and Julio!!" The voice from the older, male performer, who was apparently the leader of the troupe, bellowed throughout the street, encouraging new passersby to stop and enjoy the performance. Layla and Jeannie cheered on with the rest of the crowd. Just then, Layla's phone rang.

"Jeannie, I have to take this. I'll be right back."

Layla walked away from the crowd to a quiet area of the square so that she could hear the telephone conversation.

"Hey, baby. You finally answered. I miss you." Leon's voice was insincerely joyful.

"Leon? I thought this was Jasmine. Quit calling me."

He could hear music and voices in the distance. The realization that Layla was out on the town on a Saturday night quickly upset Leon. He wondered why she was out so late. It was only nine o'clock in Arizona.

"Who you with, girl? I know you aren't cheating on me. Hell no." His voice became sterner and louder as he spoke.

"It's none of your business, Leon. But if you must know, I'm with Jeannie from Lynwood. You know."

"That bitch!! You're going lesbian on me. I knew it. You were so friendly with my cousin, Carol. I warned you that Carol was a lesbian and that she'd try to hit on you. But you wouldn't listen. You kept being nice to her. Even my sister thought you were a lesbian. She warned me."

Leon's voice became exasperated.

"How dare you? I'm not talking about this now."

Layla hung up her phone. She gazed across the street toward Jeannie in despair.

REVELATION

NEW YORK CITY, NEW YORK

Two Weeks Later

WITH THE PASSING OF TIME, Layla remembered her promise to Jeannie to give her high school sweetheart, Roland, a chance again. In some sense, Layla unconsciously felt like she was being unfaithful to Leon if she did. But in several heartfelt calls throughout the intervening days, Jeannie reassured her that Layla wasn't in a relationship with Leon and had no commitment to him. Layla struggled with that but ultimately agreed. She then wondered how to go about reaching out to Roland without seeming desperate or without having to broach the subject of her travels to Puerto Rico with not one man but two. She was somewhat embarrassed by it all. But if she was going to move forward then she needed to leave her past behind and think about her future and her need to be loved. She could no longer think of others needs and feelings. Her priority was herself and her emotional well-being. Why not? She deserved to be loved.

Layla decided to text Roland a simple message:

"Hey, Roland. Thinking of you."

As soon as the text was sent. She regretted sending it. Maybe it was too direct? Or too subtle? Maybe she should have asked to speak to him? Maybe she should have called instead? Rather than fret over it, she focused on her day and that she had to get to work.

She took the coach bus nearest to her house in Middletown so that she could make the long, early-morning trek to her new job. After the bus, Layla took the subway, the Q train, and then a taxi to her ultimate destination at 99th Street and Madison Avenue. The hospital spanned several streets in Manhattan's Upper East Side and included various buildings on campus.

Because the commute was so long and unpredictable, Layla often arrived an hour or two before her shift. She typically ate breakfast at the cafeteria in the Guggenheim Pavilion. Fresh juice and fruit were her staples. An occasional muffin with strong coffee on those days when she was particularly tired and needed a pick-me-up. Maple pancakes when Layla had a long shift during the weekends.

Layla sat in the cafeteria alone. She browsed Facebook, liking photos of her friends in California, and reviewing the day's memories. Layla rarely posted. She posted a picture of flowers sent to her by a patient's family the previous day. Although Layla no longer provided bedside nursing anymore in the cardiothoracic ICU, she still tried to ensure that her patients' family knew that the entire staff cared, including management. Receiving beautiful flowers from a family was truly why Layla treasured being a nurse all those years. She had been feeling a little discouraged lately. The flowers uplifted her spirits. In fact, it almost brought her to tears. Seeing her friends liking her Facebook post about the flowers and making encouraging comments made her feel even more appreciated. Her friends reassured Layla that she made a difference every day in someone's life. That brought a smile to her face on such an early morning.

As Layla was about to stand up and walk to her unit, she received a text from Roland:

"Good morning sweet lady. Thinking of you too."

Her heart palpitated faster. Should she take the risk? She had to. She promised Jeannie that she would. Layla texted back:

"Are you in the city tonight? Can we meet?"

There was no immediate response. But eventually, Roland texted back: "Sure."

Uncertain how to interpret this, Layla decided to follow through and arrange a time to meet Roland.

THE SPIRALING grand ramp of the Guggenheim Museum continued endlessly until it reached the domed light at the top. Looking upwards made Layla dizzy. She was already nervous but tried to enjoy the contemporary art that filled the main gallery. However, she knew that her purpose there wasn't to enjoy the art or the Frank Lloyd Wright design. It was to meet Roland again for the first time since they saw each other at the Newark Liberty International Airport. Layla was nervous and worried. Roland was already fifteen minutes late. She was unsure whether it was because of the traffic or if he decided not to show. Roland hadn't texted her yet about his delay and Layla didn't want to seem anxious. At the very least, she could salvage the night by enjoying the museum. She comforted herself with this thought.

As she walked around near the entrance to the ramp, Roland finally arrived. He was calm and relaxed, unfazed by his lateness.

"Hey girl," he said as he approached and gave her a hug. "You look beautiful."

"Thank you." Layla was still in her work clothes, so she knew that Roland was being his flirty self without regard to the reality of the circumstances. But the flattery was still welcome.

"I'm glad we finally connected. This is a lovely place. I've never been here before," Roland said with a surprising air of confidence. He was clearly out of his element and his work clothes showed it.

"Thanks for coming. I know it's been a while, but I'm hoping that it won't be the last."

Roland smiled. The couple continued walking. They stopped in front of a still life by Paul Cezanne. In admiring the painting, Layla commented, "It's so simple yet elegant. This jug juxtaposed by the glass and fruit reminds me of spending summers with my Granny Little. I just love her."

Although unimpressed by the painting, Roland remembered Layla often speaking of Granny Little when she was a teenager. "Wow, how is she?" he asked.

"She just celebrated her ninety-fifth birthday and is still going strong. Praise God."

"That's incredible. Wish her happy birthday for me." Roland thought of the several classmates who recently passed away and wondered about his own mortality.

Roland's demeanor suddenly and unexpectedly changed.

"Listen, Layla. I have something to tell you. Something that I should have said a long time ago."

Layla's expression became blank.

"I know that we get along really well. We've known each other since we were teenagers. That means so much to me. But... But I've been living with someone."

Layla's jaw dropped. She wanted to hear first what the circumstances were, especially since she couldn't claim the high road herself.

"Roland, you can tell me. For how long?"

"Since before we first went out." The hesitation in his voice was apparent.

"Are you serious? All this time? Even when you saw me at the airport? Why didn't you say anything?"

"I wanted to. I really did. But I was breaking up with Flor and I didn't want to make more of the situation than what it really was." He wasn't sure if he had said too much or the right thing.

"Obviously, you two are still together. You're still living with her."

"Yes, we're still together. But I want to give us a chance."

"You're joking, right? I'm not gonna date a man living with another woman. What kind of woman do you think I am? I deserve better than that. Don't you think?"

"Listen, Layla. I'm not sure what's going to happen. I just want to still spend time with you and to get to know you again. If we fall in love, we fall in love."

"I'm not sneaking around with someone else's man."

"That's not what I mean. You're getting it wrong."

"That sounds like what you mean. You're not talking about breaking up with her and moving out. Even if you do, that's not what I want. I'm no rebound chick."

Layla started walking away towards the museum's exit. Roland followed.

"Wait... don't go..."

PALMDALE

PALMDALE, CALIFORNIA

Four Months Later

AFTER PAPA LITTLE closed the kitchen door to his condominium, he walked outside to the patio overlooking the arid desert of Antelope Valley. He could see the rugged San Gabriel mountains in the distance. But the breathtaking views that Sunday morning didn't distract him from his singular purpose. He dialed a disguised number on his cellphone while nervously glancing through the sliding glass patio doors to ensure that his wife wasn't within earshot.

"Hey babe, glad to hear from you." His baritone voice seduced the female caller every time she answered. Today was no different.

"Hey, handsome. When am I going to see you again? I miss you." The excited female voice only encouraged Papa Little's antics. She was one of many women on the side that he talked to despite being recently married.

"You know I miss you too." Over the years, Papa Little learned never to use a woman's name but to use terms of endearment while talking on the phone. It gave him deniability should his wife overhear the conversation. But in person, he was a charmer and very personable. His good looks and tall, slim physique were something women desired even at his age. Add to that his wit and wisdom, he was an unstoppable force from his youth. Women wanted him and he knew it. Although he claimed eight children through multiple marriages and relationships, the debonair lover had more children than he was unaware of.

He continued. "I have a couple of errands to do today. I might be able to stop by. But no promises." He always knew how to navigate difficult situations. Juggling multiple women was an almost full-time task, but he was used to it even before he got married.

"Ok babe. Just let me know if you can. I need you." The yearning in her voice betrayed the calmness that she wanted to convey despite her disappointment.

Before he could respond, another call interrupted. The caller id had another disguised name. How many disguised names were in his phone was a closely guarded secret. Papa Little switched over, abruptly ending the first call without a farewell.

"Hello. This is me." He knew this female caller would get irate that he would not acknowledge her name. But by now, it was a joke of sorts and part of the mystery of their relationship.

"It's Joan, David. You know who this is."

"It is? Of course." His squirrelly smile was inescapable if she could see it. But even he wondered if that was her real name. He could no longer remember it after all this time and after their continual cat and mouse game.

"I have bad news. I can't make it tomorrow. Liz is in town with the grandkids. She came into town without letting me know. I can't disappoint the kids. They want me to take them to Disneyland. I'm sorry."

"That's okay, babe. We can make it another day."

"She's going to be here at least a week, maybe more."

"No problem. Enjoy the grandkids and catch up with me when

you're free." His steel-trapped mind already thought of a substitute for the next day's activities. He planned to call another woman later that day. If she was not available, surely someone else was.

"Thanks, hun. You're so thoughtful."

The kitchen door creaked open and Cissy entered. She looked around for her husband. To her surprise, the tea kettle was whistling uncontrollably. She turned off the front burner and moved the kettle to the cooler, back one.

"David... David." Cissy kept walking, looking for her absent husband.

When she opened the patio door, Papa Little was nonchalantly seated on a white, Adirondack chair enjoying the desert view. He turned his head towards the opening glass door while secretly stashing his phone in his pocket.

"Hey, Cissy. Sit down." He gently patted the chair next to him reiterating his request.

She slowly approached somewhat confused, her eyes scanning the small patio and listening attentively. Her suspicions deepened but she buried them like she always did. Love wasn't the basis of their relationship. Convenience and support were. At least, that's what she told herself. Cissy was fifteen years younger than Papa Little. Just a few years older than Layla. She married him because he needed someone to grow old with who could take care of him at his age despite his playboy ways. In turn, Cissy needed the financial security that David's military pension and retirement benefits from his teaching job could bring to her life. She was still working but was irresponsible when it came to money. The occasional gambling trips to Laughlin and Las Vegas didn't help.

Their marriage, however, was becoming more of a marriage of inconvenience as the months passed. The distance from Palmdale to Long Beach where Cissy lived was well over a two-hour drive. The couple mainly saw each other on the weekends. When Papa Little learned that Cissy chose not to move in with him after their whirl-wind engagement and elopement, he was actually despondent. He never revealed his feelings about Cissy's decision to remain living in her own apartment to her or to his family. He knew that Layla and his other children wanted their father to finally settle down in his twilight years. His children would be against the marriage even more so if they knew that they were only a married couple on paper and actually lived apart. Layla and Granny Little would be the most vocal.

"When you were in the kitchen, a Dr. Choudry called for you. I tried yelling your name, but you didn't answer." Cissy tried to explain her interruption without sounding overbearing or controlling.

"Pay him no mind. He won't leave me alone. I'm surprised that he called again."

Cissy was puzzled at her husband's apparent apathy. A doctor making a personal call on a weekend was out of the ordinary. Even she knew that.

"What does he want?"

"He just wants me to schedule a workup. Nothing important." He failed to mention that Dr. Choudry was a cardiologist who had treated Papa Little for several years for a severe heart condition. "I'm not going. He wants someone to drive me to the appointment and any follow-ups."

"I told you, David. I don't have time for that. I have my own issues. My mother is still in hospice and my Auntie April is flying in from Detroit to take care of her. There's no way that I can take time off. I need my PTO for the girl's trip to Lake Havasu next month."

"I'm not asking you to take time off for me. I told you that I'm not going." Papa Little winced as he spoke but made pains to prevent his body from displaying it. It wouldn't matter whether Cissy saw his physical response or not. Her resolve was immovable.

"*I'm gonna have to explain this to Layla if she asks,*" he unconsciously surmised. Delaying the conversation with his daughter who was a cardiothoracic ICU nurse was an inevitable strategy. At the moment, however, that was far from his mind. He had more important matters to discuss.

"Where are we going for brunch? Our usually - Old Country Buffet?" he asked with a broad grin on his face.

"I told you. I can't afford that every week. It's bad enough the cost of gas to drive to Palmdale."

"No worries. I'll pay." The financial layouts were even discouraging him at this point. He wondered how long his wallet could take it.

FORGETTABLE MEMORIES

MESA, ARIZONA

Around the Same Time

Leon's sister sat in the backyard of his house with her feet dangling in the pool so that she could cool down in the sweltering Arizona heat. She had a lemonade with a dash of Tito's Homemade Vodka in her hand. Well, it was more than just a dash, but Loretta couldn't let Leon know. He would be upset if he found out that she was drinking. She knew he was strict about alcohol. But she needed some right now. Leon be damned. Her two kids were playing in the shallow end of the pool.

"Ronnie, I told you to be nice and don't play rough with your sister. She's afraid of the water."

"Ok, mom," he yelled back. "You won't let me have any fun," the twelve-year-old boy mumbled underneath his breath so his mom couldn't hear him.

"I heard that."

"I'm sorry." His voice was insincere.

"No, you're not. When we get home, I'm going to tell your father."

Loretta knew that her husband would call her later that day and insist that she give him details of the trip to Arizona. She didn't bother letting her son know that he would be in trouble by then because she wanted him to enjoy spending time with his Arizona family. Two of Leon's grandkids from his oldest son were also swimming in the pool.

Loretta got up from the pool and sat down on a chair near the porch. By then, Leon was finished with his telephone conversation with their brother, Joseph. Joseph planned on visiting later. Leon walked outside with a tray of goodies and placed them on the table near Loretta.

After sitting in the chair next to her, he said, "Beautiful day. Isn't it?"

"Oh yes. I love the Arizona heat. It reminds me of Palms Springs." Her sarcasm was obvious, but Leon knew better than to challenge his only sister. She was their mother's favorite, and everyone knew it.

"We can go to the waterpark if you like. It's not too far from here."

"No, the kids are fine. Besides, I want to avoid the crowds." She picked up a barbecued chicken wing and dipped it in the ranch dressing. Leon grabbed a mini-*chimichanga*. "Why didn't you invite mom? She would love to come see you."

Leon rolled his eyes in disgust.

"She prefers LA." He wouldn't look at his sister as he answered.

"That's a lie. She talks about wanting to visit you all the time. I didn't have the heart to tell her that I was coming for the weekend after you told me that she wasn't invited."

"You know how I feel about that, Loretta. I don't want to talk about it."

"We are going to talk about it. I'm tired of this family being split apart. You and Joseph here in Arizona. Me and momma in California."

Leon knew that once Loretta set her mind to something there was nothing that could change it, not even his eloquent speaking.

"You've been distant with momma ever since dad died. That's been ten years now. Momma won't tell me why. She probably doesn't even know."

"Oh, she knows."

"Leon, be straight with me." Loretta's glaring eyes portrayed her seriousness. She was going to get to the bottom of this and today was the day when it would be resolved. At least for her.

"I'm going to tell you, but you have to promise not to tell mom. She's going to deny it anyway."

"I swear, Leon."

"Don't swear if you don't mean it. God doesn't like liars."

Loretta knew that Leon would hold her to her word. But she also knew that she needed to talk to their mother about it if her brother's relationship with their mother was going to ever get better. She didn't mind a little white lie.

"I know. Go on." She waited eagerly for his side of the story.

Leon fidgeted for a while before he found the resolve to admit what was bothering him.

"You know how mom loves her Moscatos. She sips on a glass every day."

"So, there's nothing wrong with a little wine every day. Even the bible says so."

"Are you gonna let me speak or are you going to keep interrupting me?"

Loretta didn't apologize. She never did. But Leon could tell from her silence that she agreed not to interrupt again.

"You and Anthony were living in Germany then. That Air Force base there. Well, mom went through a time where it was more than just Moscatos. It was vodka and whiskey. A lot of hardcore drinking. She was drunk every day; throwing up, falling down the stairs, not going to work. Dad would call. Sometimes, he would call the ambulance because she was so passed out that he didn't know if she was still alive.

"Eventually, he stopped coming home at night, working late. But mom thought that he was cheating. 'Two can play that game,' I guess is what she thought. So, she started having an affair. Some guy in her office. But it was more than just him. Many guys. Who knows how many?"

Leon stopped and took a deep breath. He tried not to get emotionally involved recounting the events.

"I took a sabbatical from church. Even Joseph came with me. I tried listening to mom and tried to convince her that dad wasn't cheating. She didn't care. She wouldn't go to rehab. We tried getting her committed, but no place could take her. I even had Dr. Johnson and his wife do couples counseling for them. He treated them as his own parents. But it didn't help. Nothing did.

"And then..." Leon's voice trailed as his throat tightened. "I blame her. He wouldn't have been driving that night if she hadn't gone out with that guy. He went to get her back. Dad did everything to keep their marriage together. He was a saint. He endured as much as the prophet Hosea."

The silence was only broken by the sporadic laughter of the kids playing in the pool. The siblings ignored them.

Loretta squeezed his arm. Leon gently touched her hand; a form of kindness that he rarely shared.

"I didn't know anything about this." Loretta was both surprised and ashamed.

"You were in Europe for most of it until you came back for dad's funeral."

"Dad would want you to forgive her, Leon."

"I can't. I can't forgive her or any woman. Dad was strong but he was a fool. I would have left her the first time that I found out about the adultery. I'm never going to be a fool like he was."

Loretta remembered that Leon's divorce was around that time. She didn't know the whole story about the divorce as well.

"Is that why you haven't settled down since being with Angie?"

"I don't trust women, Loretta. Not anymore. I don't think I can anymore. Not after what happened to dad."

"Not even Layla? She seemed to really love you."

Leon was deep in thought. "I... I can't trust anyone. I know that I need help. But a part of me doesn't want help."

Loretta spoke to her brother about getting help even if it was from his mentor, Dr. Johnson.

WHY HAVE I LOST YOU?

PHOENIX, ARIZONA

Around the Same Time

"Lydia, can you hold my calls? Thanks." Daniel released the speaker-phone button on his office phone and then turned toward his computer monitors.

He heard Lydia yell from her cubicle down the hall, "Sure. I'm going on my break. See you in a half-hour." She took her handbag and walked to the front door.

Daniel failed to respond. Lydia was a trusted legal assistant and a workaholic. He often relied upon her to not only organize his schedule, but he also bounced off legal strategies with her when he came to an impasse. Today was different. It was a hot, Friday afternoon. Daniel should have left the office early so that he could avoid the traffic. But he forgot. A lot was on his mind lately. If he drove home now, then he would be right in the middle of heavy, rush-hour traffic with an even longer drive home. That was the last thing that he wanted to do. So, he had to figure out what to do to pass the time. He didn't feel like working for the next hour.

He tried reading a legal magazine but there weren't any articles addressing his legal specialty. He checked his iPhone. No one had texted him all day so there was no needed response. After scanning his Facebook newsfeed, nothing really interested him. He was in a malaise of sorts. Daniel needed a pick-me-up, but nothing seemed to come to mind. Besides Lydia, no one else was still in the office. So, there was no one else to talk to. He contemplated calling Jose Luis, but that was out of the question too. Daniel didn't feel like listening to a three-hour conversation with his brother about nothing. Certainly, Jose Luis wouldn't appreciate his lack of interest either. It was best to avoid a potential argument.

He decided to rest his head back on his large, leather chair and closed his eyes. His mind was racing faster than ever. Flashes of visions from arguments with opposing counsel, meetings with clients, and the *Yokahu* Tower spun in his head. He didn't want to think about work or past conversations. A power nap wasn't going to help. So, he quickly opened his eyes.

Daniel decided to check his personal email. A few spam emails weren't filtered so he deleted them. The typical sales emails from Best Buy, Nest, Home Depot, and a host of other businesses filled his inbox. He deleted those as well. However, there were no emails from any friends or family. That disappointed him. Not that people emailed often. Texting was the preferred means of communication. But the lack of something personal displeased him. He felt distant from the world, his friends, and family. He needed to do something to change that.

It had been years since Daniel wrote a letter. He thought about writing Layla a letter about what happened in Puerto Rico. Daniel's handwriting suffered after he fractured his right hand shadowboxing as a kid. Most of the time, Daniel couldn't read his own handwriting. He didn't think Layla could either unless he took significant time to handwrite the letter so that it was legible. He didn't have enough time left before he had to leave the office. Besides, he remembered that he never had her home address. Writing was out of the question.

Fortunately, Daniel remembered that he had Layla's email address. He clicked on the "new mail" button to compose an email. He was first stumped with the subject line.

He typed, "Good afternoon." That seemed impersonal so he deleted it. He typed, "Thinking of you" and paused. Would that be enough? Was it expressive enough of his feelings? Perhaps? But he wanted somehow to convey what he truly felt. He wanted something to catch Layla's heart and soul should she decide to not open the email or heaven forbid delete it. He tapped his hand on his desk repeatedly and pondered deeply until it came to him.

"Why Have I Lost You?"

She would surely understand what he meant. Did she feel the same way too? What it a loss for her? Or was it a burden unloaded? Daniel really didn't know. He wondered why Layla never reached out to him after Puerto Rico. Maybe she was so happy with Leon? Maybe she wanted Daniel to take the first step? He was after all the male and should show initiative if he wanted Layla in his life. That's how she always explained it to him when they spoke about her expectations about relationships over the years. Daniel was uncertain what Layla was thinking or feeling. It was a mystery to him.

If he spoke to his sister, Maria, she would tell him to stop thinking about her because Layla made her choice and it wasn't Daniel. If he spoke to his brother, Jose Luis, he would say the same thing. Everyone he knew would counsel him to move on and find another love. But it wasn't easy. He wanted to give their relationship a chance again or at least find out if Layla was willing to give them a chance again. To do that, he had to be honest with himself. But most of all honest with Layla. He started composing the email:

~~Dear Layla,~~
Dearest Layla,

I've missed you, especially your ~~sexy~~ voice and your laugh. I miss your smile. I miss the way that you greeted me every day with a "~~good morning~~" text and our phone calls at night before bed. I miss the way you were excited to talk to me and share with me about the patients you worked with that day. I miss the encouragement that you gave me when I was down, and I had no one to talk to me. I miss talking about traveling to ~~Puerto Rico~~ Jamaica or the Dominican Republic and the plans we made.

I wish that it didn't end ~~this way~~. I know that I was wrong for pushing him ~~Leon~~. I let my anger get the best of me. I'm sorry for embarrassing you and putting you in a position to fear for your safety. I understand that it was wrong. I hope you can forgive me. Forgive me for that and the choices that I made. I know that I don't deserve you. But if you have it in your heart to forgive me and move past what happened, please do. Please give ~~me~~ us another chance. I don't want to lose you again.

~~Love,~~
Sincerely,

Daniel

DANIEL PAUSED. He read and re-read the email over and over again. It felt right but at the same time, it felt wrong. A part of him was embarrassed to say these things. A part of him was afraid of rejection.

He didn't know how Layla would receive the email. Daniel noticed that the email had too many "I"s in it. It read as if he was being selfish and self-centered and thinking only about his own feelings. He thought that Layla may be offended by that. He contemplated re-writing the email focusing on her feelings rather than his. But he realized that it would take time and the hour had already passed. He needed to head home. So, he quickly pushed the delete button. Or so it seemed.

LAYLA'S IPHONE DINGED. She glanced at it and saw a notification: "Email received from Daniel Mendoza."

SIPPING COFFEE

MIDDLETOWN, NEW YORK

Around the Same Time

WHEN LAYLA SAW the notification on her iPhone, she wondered whether to delete the email. Why didn't Daniel call her? Why did he send an email of all things and not a text? Those thoughts and others crossed her mind. She struggled with being upset at him and offended. But Amirah's words surfaced repeatedly: "The happiest that I've seen you, mom, is when you're with Daniel. Even when you are just talking about him, you glow like a teenager." Layla was surprised that just the thought of Amirah's comments made her smile. But the smile quickly turned into a frown. She wished that she hadn't received the email because it meant that she had to deal with something that she avoided for a long time, but she was certainly curious about it.

"*I'll read it when I get home,*" she thought. It was more like she was trying to convince herself.

The coach bus jiggled a bit as it hit potholes. Layla almost dropped her phone in the seat next to her. Unfortunately, the elderly gentleman who normally sat next to her wasn't riding the bus that night. He was visiting his family in New Orleans. That commonality made talking to him easier for Layla; although she was normally very outgoing even with total strangers. Most thought that she was aloof because Layla never left home without a pair of Airpods in her ears. The Airpods drowned out the noise but not Layla's interest in her surroundings and the diverse people residing in New York from all over the world. Without her bus partner to talk to that early evening, Layla decided to reach out to one of her friends to pass the time.

Layla typed fast when she texted. It was probably from her typing class in high school when she could type like the whirlwind on a Selectric II. Her thumbs typed fiercely because texting was now her preferred means of communication. She never explained why because, when raising her children, she constantly proclaimed the intimacy of personal conversation.

"Guess who I heard from." The text zipped onto her screen and then was sent to her best friend in Dallas with lightning speed.

"Girl, please. Not Leon again. When is he gonna give it up?" Layla could hear Jeannie's voice in her head as she read the text.

"No, not him. Daniel. What do you think?"

"Seriously? That's a surprise."

"I know."

Layla had told Jeannie about Roland's proposition. Jeannie secretly felt ashamed of her advice to Layla. She was disappointed at his revelation, but she reassured Layla that she was doing the right thing. Layla deserved better than being a side chick with the hopes of being more someday. Jeannie knew, as well as Layla, that those relationships never last. Roland made his choice even if it was unconscious. Flor was that choice. But Jeannie was surprised that the one person who she thought had given up actually reached out.

At least Daniel was somewhat of a nerd and a homebody. So, Layla knew that he was not the type of man who had several women at once. In fact, dealing with women was difficult for him. Strong and opinionated women like Layla took all of Daniel's efforts to be socially graceful. But try as he may, Daniel seemed more confident when he was with Layla. Even she sensed it. That pleased her.

"What are you going to do?" Jeannie asked.

The question was expected. Even Layla didn't know what her response would be; at least not at that point. She became extremely pensive but decided to be honest. That always worked for her in the past when talking with Jeannie.

"I haven't read his email yet. It depends on what he says. Don't know what he's thinking."

"Let me know what you decide."

"I will girl. Thanks for listening."

"Any time."

◊ ◊ ◊

AFTER ARRIVING HOME, Layla sat on her front porch with both feet on the wood railing, looking out towards her neighbors' homes across the street. The night sky was glowing with stars, illuminating her neighborhood which was light-pollution free, unlike the city. There were no archaic streetlamps. The only artificial lighting was the single porch light on each home which were situated on half-acre lots. The cooler summer air whisked around her body, slightly chilling her. She snuggled her jacket tighter and sipped from her coffee mug using the heat to also slightly warm her hands.

Her iPhone sat on her lap secretly gnawing at her. She had not deleted the lock screen notification indicating the email sent from Daniel. It appeared every time the iPhone was jostled, a subtle reminder that she should read it and face the inevitable. Maybe a text or phone call would follow if she didn't respond. But Layla knew that Daniel was not persistent like Leon. This may be his only effort to reach out to her. She reached for her cellphone but was interrupted.

"Good evening, lovely lady." Layla looked up as her female neighbor, Mrs. Mumphrey, opened the front door to her house directly across from Layla's house.

"Good evening, Penelope."

"I saw you sitting outside. It's a lovely night."

"Yes, it is."

"Anyway, Byron asked me to find out if you need him to mow your lawn again. He says that it's looking mighty tall."

Mr. Mumphrey had been mowing Layla's lawn since her son, Kalvin, went to boot camp in Hawaii two years earlier. Layla appreciated his kindness even though she could mow the lawn herself like she used to do when Kalvin was away at summer camps or visiting her family in California. She only acceded to Mr. Mumphrey's request because he was a retiree who had little to do now that his sons and only daughter moved to the Mid-west.

"Thank you. Tell Byron that I would appreciate that. I always appreciate his help." Layla sipped more coffee.

"I will. Have a good night."

"Goodnight, Penelope."

Mrs. Mumphrey entered her home almost allowing the door to slam shut before she caught it. She grinned at Layla recognizing her clumsiness.

When Mrs. Mumphrey was no longer in sight, Layla glanced at her iPhone again. Before long, Layla read Daniel's wordy email. It was unlike him to be so vulnerable, but she was familiar with his apologetic ways. Daniel had told her that for years, well into his adulthood, he never apologized because Daniel never felt like he was ever in the wrong. He learned the hard way that his arrogance sabotaged his relationships, including his former marriage with Christina. After that, he took pains to ensure that he acknowledged his errant ways and apologize for them. Layla thought that Daniel may have overcompensated at times by apologizing for things that he was not at fault for; perhaps in an effort to smooth over the relationship and end any conflict. But the apology in his email seemed sincere and genuine.

Layla was surprised when Daniel left the Wyndham Grand Rio Mar hotel on the day after their visit to the *El Yunque* rainforest. Another inconsiderate man would have insisted that she leave and get her own hotel room if, like Daniel, they had paid for the entire trip including the accommodations. On top of that, Layla just realized that Daniel let her keep the rental car for the rest of her stay and probably had to pay a significant fee to change to an earlier flight back to Phoenix. It never dawned on her how things changed after meeting Leon. Layla and Leon never spoke about the incident after it happened. She wondered why.

Now that she had stopped seeing Leon, Layla tried to view the incident with different eyes, more objectively. Could Leon have been in the wrong? That never occurred to her at the time or since her return from Puerto Rico. She saw what she saw but, sitting on her porch that evening, she acknowledged to herself for the first that she wasn't present the whole time and didn't know how it really began. She also remembered that she never gave Daniel the opportunity to explain his side of the story. Maybe she should have out of fairness?

BIRTHDAY

MIDDLETOWN, NEW YORK

The Same Night

Layla was certain that she needed to do something to rectify the situation with Daniel. She contemplated calling Jeannie for advice but was concerned that Jeannie would convince her to let it go and find a man in New York. Any discouraging words were not needed at that moment. Besides, Layla agreed to tell Jeannie what she decided to do after reading Daniel's email. Layla never agreed to let Jeannie know what she decided before she actually acted upon it. That brought Layla a sense of justification and relief for not immediately calling Jeannie and letting her know that she was going to call Daniel.

Fortunately, Layla hadn't deleted Daniel's number in her iPhone. She called and anxiously awaited whether there would be an answer. She quickly remembered that Daniel was three hours behind New York's time zone. By the time she made up her mind and placed the phone call, it was still early evening in Arizona.

"He should be home," she thought. *"I hope he's home."* When

the call was not answered after the third ring, *"What if he's not home. Should I leave a voicemail? What should I say? No, it's better if he hears my voice when we talk. He'll call me back."* She reassured herself that, after seven years, she knew Daniel well enough to know that he was honorable and would not act out of spite; at least not towards her. He had never done so in the past. He surely would take her call even though they had not spoken in a long time.

"Hello," Daniel's voice echoed from the Bluetooth connection in his car. The sound of wind whipping around Daniel's car as he sped down the interstate highway towards home could be heard in the background.

"Hi, Daniel. It's me, Layla."

"It's good to hear your voice again." Daniel slightly grinned. He was surprised that Layla had called. She had made no efforts to speak with him since Puerto Rico. And frankly, he knew that he was no better. He regretted not reaching out himself.

"I got your email. Thanks for apologizing."

A surprised look took over his entire face. *"I must have accidentally sent it,"* he thought. After deciding not to admit that fact, Daniel responded, "You're welcome. I'm truly sorry, Layla. I know you deserve better and you deserve an explanation."

"No apologies necessary. We were in a difficult situation."

"I know. I'm sorry that we had to go through that. I really believed that we were having a great time in Puerto Rico together. Wish it didn't end."

"So why didn't you call me?"

"Honestly, I was hurt that you chose him. And besides, you made your choice. I didn't want to interfere. You have a long history with him." Daniel hated saying Leon's name, especially when talking with Layla. When he discussed his relationship with Layla with others, Daniel would easily speak his name. He felt that acknowledging Leon's name to Layla would uncover her emotions for him. That was the last thing that Daniel wanted. "I understand why it may be difficult for you to let go. I wanted you to choose me. Nothing I said or did would change that."

"I'm sorry too, Daniel."

"I hope you're happy, Layla. I really am. You mean the world to me. Although, I wanted to be the one to make you happy. I really did." Daniel pressed his hand against his chest so that Layla couldn't hear his deep sigh.

"I'm no longer with Leon. We left Puerto Rico separately," Layla said nervously wondering how Daniel would take the revelation. "It's never going to work. He has anger management issues."

Daniel knew that all along because Layla had mentioned that to him before they dated. He was surprised, however, that she still choice Leon despite her knowledge of these issues. Daniel was not aware of any physical abuse. Layla hid that from him just like she hid it from Jeannie and all of her other friends and family members. Daniel pondered what to say that wouldn't come across as being arrogant or unsympathetic.

"I'm so sorry, Layla." He wondered if even this simple statement came across as callous or opportunistic.

"Thank you, Daniel. But enough about me. How have you been?"

"I've been busy with work."

"I know. I saw your post about your trial. Congratulations."

"Thank you. It was a moral victory. I was hoping for a defense verdict. A small part of me was. But the plaintiff was asking for one point nine million dollars. In the end, he only received a hundred and sixty-five thousand dollars. That was about what we last offered to settle the case. So, my client was pleased."

"Nice job."

"Thanks. It takes a lot out of me. Fourteen plus hour days. I can't really sleep. I need a vacation again," Daniel laughed. He wasn't sure how Layla would take this comment, so he quickly changed the topic. "I saw that Jeannie visited you. How was Hamilton?"

"It was fun. I was surprised. I didn't realize that the play had a lot

of hip-hop and rap music. Don't get me wrong. It had some traditional music typically in plays like *Les Mis* and Phantom of the
Opera, but most of it was hip-hop music. It's no wonder why it's so
popular. I think you will like it. Have you seen a play on Broadway?"

"No, I haven't. London, yes, but not New York. I've always
wanted to see it on Broadway. I hear it's great."

Daniel was happy that the conversation developed beyond their
encounter with Leon in Puerto Rico. It gave him hope.

"You should see it. Broadway is a different experience."

"That's what I hear. It's been years since I went to New York.
Last time, I had the opportunity to visit Times Square, but I didn't
have time for a play."

"Well, you should visit me, and we can go. I can show you the
city in a way you've never seen. I'll be your personal guide this time."
Layla chuckled. She knew that when Daniel visited her the one time
in the past, they hung out at her house and enjoyed Upstate New
York. She believed that visiting the city could be a different experience that may bring them closer.

"I would really love that."

"Isn't your birthday coming up? We've never been together for
your birthday." Layla hoped that remembering Daniel's birthday
would let down his guard.

"Yes, it is. Next month."

"Take a few days off of work and make it a long weekend. Come
visit me. We can have fun together."

"That will be nice. Let me check with my assistant to see if I have
any appointments around my birthday. She forgets and always sched-
ules some on my birthday if I don't remind her not to."

"Sure, let me know."

"I will. I do want to come see you, so if Lydia scheduled something then I'll have her reschedule it. I just need to first check to see if
it can be rescheduled."

That response made Layla feel like Daniel was being sincere and
not just being cordial.

After his response, there was a pause in their conversation. Layla could hear another song playing in the background in Daniel's car. She asked, "Are you listening to Cameo? Is that 'Why Have I Lost You'?"

"Yes, I love this song."

"I always loved that song too. So deep and emotional."

"Yes, it is. It's surprising how songs nowadays don't express sorrow and loss."

"Exactly," Layla was pleased that they had this in common. She never knew that about Daniel.

"When I wanna blues it about a beautiful Creole girl that I lost (who's living in Middletown) then I play this song."

"Wow. Just go ahead and pull at my heart strings."

Daniel thought, *That's what I want to do, sweetheart.* A part of him wanted to say that to Layla aloud. Instead, he said, "Well, I did lose you."

CONFRONTATION

MESA, ARIZONA

A Week Later

"You don't say." Leon was obviously irritated by the caller's comments. "How did you find out?"

"I saw it on my newsfeed last night."

"Did Layla use his name?"

"She didn't. Her post was vague. Something about some male coming to visit her from out of state."

Leon knew that he was no longer friends with Layla on Facebook and could not check the post himself. But Marlo was a trusted friend who had provided Leon with valuable information about Layla many times in the past including that Layla was vacationing in Puerto Rico with Daniel. He had no reason to doubt Marlo. She had been friends with Layla since their senior year in high school and became friends with Leon once Layla started dating him. Because she was still friends with Layla on Facebook, Marlo could see all of her private posts. Layla was none the wiser.

"Can you message her and ask who it is and why he's coming to visit?" Leon was anxious to know who this new man was in Layla's life and whether he was serious competition or a fleeting fling.

"I never message Layla. She'll be suspicious if I do. We aren't that close."

Disappointed that Marlo wouldn't take his suggestion and stealthily investigate on his behalf, Leon frantically thought of alternatives that she would accept. "Can you screenshot the post and text it to me?"

"Sure. I'll do that right now."

"Thanks, babe. I really appreciate you," Leon said with his debonair voice that he often used to manipulate her and other women.

Marlo became gleeful. She always admired Leon and his spiritual walk with God. He was a strong Pastor with an intimate congregation who he mentored over the decades. She was flabbergasted that Layla wanted nothing to do with him anymore. What woman wouldn't want such a handsome man of God? Marlo couldn't deny that she would love to be his First Lady. Maybe that's why she did everything that she could to earn his trust. One day, Marlo believed, Leon would come to truly appreciate her and see that he was wasting his time on Layla. That day was not coming soon enough for Marlo's liking.

When Leon finally received the picture of Layla's post, it verified his worst fear, causing him to become more despondent. "I can't believe this. I've done everything for this woman and now this." Leon hadn't realized that he was speaking aloud such that Marlo could hear him.

"You don't deserve this, Leon."

Her unexpected response bewildered him until he realized what happened.

"No. No, I don't." Leon didn't want to openly admit that he loved Layla. At least, he believed that he did even though the therapy sessions that he recently started with Dr. Johnson made him question those feelings.

"What are you going to do?" Marlo asked Leon this same question many times before. Somehow, she expected a different answer and a different outcome. But today was no different.

"I'm going to do what I always do. I'm the man and I have my needs and desires too."

Anxious to look further into the mystery man, Leon quickly ended the conversation so that he could analyze the post even further. Marlo's fading voice could be heard, "Call me later." But Leon didn't pay attention to her words. Instead, he skimmed the comments to the post hoping to find something revealing.

In less than a day, the post garnered thirty-four likes, twelve hearts, and two sad faces. The two males who responded with sad faces also indicated their displeasure that Layla was spending time with another man. One, in particular, posted "I will have your heart one day and, from that day on, your lips and soul will smile." Leon noticed that Layla liked the post and responded with a heart. He was infuriated with her obvious flirtation with yet another man. *How could she?*" he thought.

Leon kept reading comments from Layla's female friends. Most were congratulatory until he came across Jeannie's comment: "I'm surprised, pretty lady. Glad you worked it out after the events of PR." Then it dawned on him. Layla was seeing Daniel again.

WHEN SHE RAN BACK to her master bedroom so that she could answer her iPhone, Layla almost slipped on the floor because the water dripping from her body made the tile slippery. In her haste, she forgot to turn off the shower. The large white towel haphazardly wrapped around her body loosened slightly as she ran. The call was unexpected and the caller unrevealed given the generic ringtone that played. But somehow Layla was anxious to answer it even so far as to abruptly end her ritualistic evening shower. In her mind, she believed that it may be a call from Daniel. Her heart raced at the thought.

"Hello," her subtle sexy voice almost shivered as she spoke, but not from the cold.

"Hey, baby."

Layla checked her phone to determine why Leon's photo did not appear on the screen. If it did, she wouldn't have answered. But Leon slyly called from an unknown number. A burner that he typically reserved for his side chicks or female friends like Marlo. He had never called Layla before from it. Because she wasn't answering his calls, this was his last option; one that he desperately had to take.

"Oh my god, Leon. I've had enough of this."

She was about to hang up and he anticipated that.

"Wait a minute. Don't you dare hang up on me! After all that we've been through, I deserve to be heard." Originally, his voice grew louder but tapered off at the end. "I want... I need to apologize; to you and to everyone else. I've apologized to my mom." That was a bald face lie but Layla wouldn't know. "Are you going to at least give me the opportunity to apologize to you?"

Layla tried to remain calm. It took all of her might not to curse him out. When he realized that she was still on the call, he began anew.

"Thank you." His voice lowered by an octave. "I haven't been the best. I've done things to hurt you. Horrible things that I am ashamed of. That you didn't deserve. You were the only woman who was there for me unconditionally. No one has ever treated me that way. I was too scared, too ashamed to let you know, to be vulnerable to you. I was afraid that it would end, that it was all a lie, but it wasn't. I'm sorry for not trusting you."

"Although I appreciate your apology, it's too late, too late for us."

Leon confessed that he was doing therapy with his former mentor. Layla listened attentively to how many times he met with Dr. Johnson, what they discussed, and some of the breakthroughs that he struggled with. Leon held back his hurt feelings involving his parents. He wanted to save that for a different day when they could speak in person.

"I'm a new man, Layla. And I have a future and a hope for us."

"I don't know what to say, Leon. I'm happy for you, but I've moved on. You need to move on too."

Suddenly, he became angry again. "I know you're with Daniel again. He's coming to visit you in New York. Isn't he?"

"What? Who told you that?"

"I have my sources."

Layla wondered if Leon figured out her passwords and opened up her messages on Facebook.

"You're stalking me now? You're not a new man like you say."

"God told me that we're meant for each other. You're making a mistake asking Daniel to visit you. God's not gonna bless that relationship. It's not what He wants. He wants us to be together."

"Leon..."

"I truly believe that. Just so you know how serious I am, I'll come visit you in New York. Tell me that's what you want, and I'll be there tomorrow."

In all the years that they had been dating, Leon never visited Layla or even showed any interest in visiting her. He always said that his church came first and, if she wanted to be with him, then she needed to travel to Arizona. Layla was jolted by his offer. It seemed sincere, but disingenuous at the same time.

ECG

PALMDALE, CALIFORNIA

The Next Day

THE WHEELS ROLLED WILDLY as the metal gurney was pushed from the red and white ambulance into the emergency room of the Palmdale Regional Medical Center. Flapping in the wind was the clinically white sheet covering the patient, occasionally revealing the patient's bare skin and exposing him to the elements. The double glass doors rattled as they automatically opened when the gurney along with two male paramedics neared the entrance. It was unexpectedly quiet with few patients in the waiting area. A Hispanic female nurse, dressed in blue scrubs with the name of the hospital emblazoned in black, quickly approached.

"We have a black male in his sixties with a probable myocardial infarction." The younger paramedic told the nurse who then motioned where the gurney should be directed; a small hovel in the side of the emergency room near the rear. The pale blue curtains were pushed aside to allow the gurney to enter.

"Where am I? Where am I?" the confused patient muttered. His eyes were glazed.

"What's his name?" the nurse asked as she pushed the brake on the metal casters on her side of the gurney to ensure that it stayed in place.

The second, more-seasoned paramedic replied, "We don't know. A neighbor called 911 and the patient has been incoherent. He didn't have any identification on him."

"Sir, what's your name?" the nurse directed the questions to the semi-conscious patient.

"My name... my name?" He was still confused and fatigued but struggled to remember. "David. My name is David Little."

◊ ◊ ◊

Several hours later, Papa Little was on the seventh floor of the cardiac care unit in a semi-private room. Snoring came from the other side of the white curtain separating the room from another elderly patient who was deep in sleep. Papa Little tried desperately to ignore it and focus on a golf magazine in his hands. He let the magazine drop to his lap when three doctors unexpectedly entered the room.

"Hello, Mr. Little. This is Dr. Hastings and Dr. Tahir," said Dr. Choudhry, the lead cardiologist for the hospital.

"Good morning, doctors." Although weakened, Papa Little was still his chipper self. His throat was a little sore.

Dr. Choudhry walked bedside and stood over him. The other doctors followed. "We have the results of your latest echocardiogram. Unfortunately, I have bad news. Your heart is now only pumping at only sixteen percent. That's a big drop from your last ECG. We have talked about this before. You're at Stage D. We seriously need to discuss your options."

"What are they, doctor?" Papa Little tried to hide the seriousness of his question with his typical, beaming smile.

He had seen Dr. Choudhry several times over the past few years for consults on his heart and was familiar with him but not the other doctors. Dr. Choudhry was somewhat concerned with Papa Little's nonchalant demeanor and decided to press upon him the seriousness of the situation.

"Well, we talked about a heart transplant before or a mechanical heart pump. But those options are no longer available."

Papa Little squirmed while he sat up higher on the hospital bed. He raised his right hand to touch the top of his forehead and looked down. He wanted to avoid looking at the doctors out of a sense of guilt and shame.

"I know this is disappointing news. We've wanted to put you on the transplant list but without your cooperation, there's nothing that we can do. We can offer you end-of-life care. There's a local hospice near here. We can transfer you there if you'd like."

"No, Doc. I want to go home. I prefer to be with family." His resolute voice surprised even himself. But a song of confidence began coursing through him.

"Ok, if that's what you want. We can provide services at your home as well. We will need to observe you for a few hours before you can be discharged." Doctor Choudhry wrote some notes on the iPad that he carried with him. He then clicked a few icons on the app indicating the patient's decision. "Do you have someone who can pick you up?"

"I can ask my family, but they live in Long Beach."

"Well, let me know if you want me to call them. Dr. Hastings or Dr. Tahir will still be here when you're ready to be discharged. They can speak to your family in person if you like. Just push the call nurse button so that they can let one of the doctors know."

The doctors exited the hospital room and a CTICU nurse entered to check on Papa Little.

SELF-CONDEMNATION

PALMDALE, CALIFORNIA

Later That Day

"Um, um. Why didn't you tell Layla? She knows what to do. That's her specialty, David." Grandma Little expressed her disgust and disappointment in a way that made her youngest son feel like a child again. "You're lucky I'm here in Long Beach. Otherwise, I'd make you get me a switch and whoop your behind. I'm not playing, boy."

"I know, Mama. I'm going to tell her."

"You'd better, before I do. If I have to, then she will be really upset at you. Have you told any of your kids?"

"No, Mama. I'm not sure I want to. There's nothing they can do."

"They'll want to see their father before he dies. That's why. You ain't gonna keep that from them. Are you?"

Granny Little knew that her son wasn't truly close to any of his kids. Sure, he spoke with them on occasion and hung out with them on those days when they were in town, but he mostly spent time with the various women in his life. His kids were an afterthought even at his age. He had been this way his entire life. With only a few days left, a week or two at the most, Granny Little thought that her son would be focused on spending time with family; the people who truly matter. A part of her knew that she was asking too much, but why shouldn't she expect the most of her son? She always held him to a higher standard so that he would find it in himself to become a better person, a better father. He fell short most of the time. She continued encouraging him no matter what. When he didn't fail and he rose to the occasion that surprised her, but she did not let him know about her doubts. Instead, she always focused on the positive.

"I just need peace. I don't need drama in my life right now."

"If you wanted peace, then you wouldn't have married that woman. She's too young for you." Papa Little was also used to the scolding and vehement disapproval of his life choices.

"Mama now isn't the time for all this. I need my rest."

"Okay, baby. I'll be praying for you. Remember the Lord can do miracles. Just believe that. You need to pray too."

"I will, Mama. Love you."

"Love you too."

ABOUT AN HOUR LATER, Papa Little anxiously dialed his oldest daughter.

"Babygirl, it's good to hear your voice. How are you doing?"

Layla knew something was wrong. Her father rarely called and certainly not while she was at work.

"I'm doing fine, dad. How are you?" Layla stopped talking to one of her newer nurses about a patient who just got out of surgery and walked to her office in the back. She closed the door so that she could focus on her father. Her staff knew not to disturb her when the door was closed.

"I'm good."

"Are you sure? You can tell me, Papa." Layla didn't want to give up asking her father about the real reason for his call. He often changed the topic when she inquired about him in the past. But when Layla called her father "Papa", he could not resist. She saved that ploy for dire circumstances such as this.

"Well, I have some bad news. I'm sorry."

He proceeded to tell Layla about his congestive heart failure and his admittance into the hospital the day before.

"Dad, you know I do this for a living. I can help. I can check to see if you are on the transplant waiting list."

"I'm not on the list."

"Why not?"

"It wouldn't help me. I'm too far gone."

"Don't say that. My doctor, Dr. Shapiro, he is the best in the country. He lectures all around the country and even Europe. You'd like him. I can talk to him about transferring you to my hospital where he can help you."

"You can do that for me?"

"Of course, I can. Anything for you, Dad."

Papa Little was surprised at the efforts Layla was willing to go for him even though deep inside he knew that it may not work.

"Thanks, Babygirl. I love you."

"I love you too, Dad." Layla's eyes welled up with tears. She realized the gravity of the situation.

"I should have visited you more in New York and seen my grandkids. How is Cadence?" Papa Little's voice failed as he tried to hold back tears.

"She's growing big. She's so smart. Smarter than me. You'd be so proud of your great granddaughter when you finally meet her. Jasmine would like that."

Layla knew that her father had not seen her children since they were young. She often traveled by herself to California to visit family especially in recent years after her children entered their teenage years. Her children had no desire to vacation in California and were too busy involved in their own relationships. So, her children never developed a close relationship with their grandfather or the rest of Layla's family on the West Coast. If anything, Layla regretted not instilling that in her children. But if she could convince her father to move to New York for treatment, maybe that would make up for her mistake.

WORRISOME

GILBERT, ARIZONA

A Few Hours Later

When Daniel rolled over one more time, he looked at his alarm clock and noticed that only nine minutes had passed since he last looked at it. It was now 3:24 a.m. and he was still having difficulty sleeping even though it was an early Saturday morning. His mind was racing as usual. He tried to suppress thoughts of work: discovery that he needed to propound, experts to retain, depositions to take. No matter how much he tried to think of something else, it kept coming back to work.

"Oh God, please help me sleep," he muttered audibly even though no one could hear him.

Daniel pulled the covers over his head as a way to keep the glowing green LED light from his alarm clock from glaring in his eyes when he tossed and turned. But that just made things worse.

Reluctantly, Daniel rose from the bed and walked to the pantry. He opened a bottle and took two tablets of melatonin in hopes that it would help him sleep. But the pills never worked. It was a daily, unwelcome routine that Daniel woke up automatically after sleeping for four hours no matter when he originally went to bed. He never knew why.

Before lying back down, Daniel picked up his iPad from his nightstand and checked his text messages. The typical morning greeting from Layla was missing. He wondered why. But rather than just ignoring it, he texted her: "Good morning, sweetheart. Hope you're doing well."

After looking at his alarm clock once more, he thought to himself, "Its 6:39 in Middletown. Layla should be up already." He knew that she either stayed up all night because her internal clock had changed from having worked the graveyard shift for twenty years or she woke up early to prepare for work. Either way, Daniel knew that he was not waking her up and that she would not be perturbed by the early morning text.

He stared at the iPad desperately awaiting her response. He continued staring but nothing was forthcoming. Realizing that the glow from the iPad would keep him up, Daniel closed his eyes. Inevitably, he fell asleep again even if it was only a half-hearted sleep.

SEVERAL HOURS later when Daniel groggily woke up, he checked his iPad again. Still no text from Layla. Daniel thought it was strange. She typically responded within the hour. *"Perhaps, she's busy at work,"* he thought. He decided to leave it alone. *"She will text or call when she has free time."*

After showering and making himself some lox and bagels, Daniel walked to his backyard and sat down on his daybed. He placed his food and a glass of orange juice on the bronze, wicker side table near the daybed. Reclining against the beige and cocoa pillows, he listened to music on his iPad and checked his Facebook. He posted birthday wishes to fellow classmates from high school and liked a few comments but noticed that nothing had been posted by Layla. She would normally post about going to the gym or running in the neighborhood on her days off. Occasionally, she would post about her only grandchild.

Again, he ignored the lack of posting despite a nagging feeling in his gut that something was wrong. Oftentimes, Daniel felt something happened to his family and friends and it turned out to be nothing. He attributed this slight paranoia to the nature of his legal career dealing with people who died or were severely injured because of unsuspecting life circumstances.

Rather than focus on the negative, Daniel decided to look up things to do in New York City. He was anxious to see the city and the numerous touristy things to do. Top of his list of things to do was to visit the 9/11 memorial at the World Trade Center. He also googled the Statue of Liberty and the Empire State Building. Before he got too enthralled with planning an entire itinerary for his upcoming visit to Layla for his birthday weekend, Daniel remembered that there was a possibility that Layla already had a full weekend planned. He didn't want to upstage her or give the appearance that they had to do the activities that he pre-selected. Being open-minded and flexible would be the best strategy. Besides, having lived in New York for most of her adult life, Daniel suspected that Layla was more familiar with what they could do to have fun and what exciting activities were off the beaten path that he could not find on the Internet.

By the time Daniel came to this realization, it was nearly 11 a.m. He had to run some errands before the day got away from him. So, he got into his car and drove to the mall.

When Daniel finally crawled into bed around 10:45 p.m. that same night, he reached for his iPad and noticed that he inadvertently missed a text from Layla: "I'm fine. How are you?" Fortunately, he had only received it ten minutes early. He didn't want to give Layla the impression that he was playing tit for tat and wasn't responding because she hadn't responded earlier.

Daniel put on his glasses so that his eyes could focus while reading the iPad because his master bedroom was fully dark. He typed a response: "Glad to hear that you are doing well. I had a long day relaxing and running errands."

He was pleased that she finally responded even though most of that Saturday passed.

"I had a long day too" was her response. "I don't feel like typing it all out. Can we talk about it tomorrow? I'll give you a call."

"Sure, sweetheart. Get some rest."

"Thank you. Goodnight."

"Goodnight, sweetheart." Layla liked this last text and a thumbs up icon appeared.

Feeling relieved, Daniel took off his glasses, put away his iPad, and lay quietly in bed waiting to fall asleep.

CONTEMPLATION

MIDDLETOWN, NEW YORK

The Next Morning

"Granny, I don't know what to say. I'm shocked. I can't believe that she is acting that way." Layla stood up and walked to her living room. She pushed aside the curtain and looked out the large window facing the street to see if her neighbor, Mr. Mumphrey, was still mowing her front yard. She could no longer hear the boisterous sound of the lawnmower inside of her house but on occasion, it sounded like someone was talking. When she was satisfied that he was working and could not hear her telephone conversation, she continued. "Do you want me to call her?"

"Layla, dear, I don't know if that will do any good. She is a heartless woman. She won't even visit David at the hospice."

"Are you serious? Why not?"

"She's too busy. That's what she says when I can finally get a hold of her. Most of the time she won't answer her phone."

"Has Auntie Rose gone to daddy's house to pick up his things?"

"She can't. That woman changed the locks. She won't let anyone in."

"What is she afraid of?"

"She's afraid that will take everything and that she won't get anything when David dies."

"That greedy..." Layla held back once she remembered that she was talking to her grandmother and that she would not appreciate such foul language. Granny Little was a Christian and raised all of her children, including Layla, in the church. "I'm so mad, Granny. I can't believe this."

"I know dear. I've asked her to bring him food and visit often so that he isn't alone. The staff treats you better when they know family visits. I visit every day myself if I could still drive. Just so you know, I had Marcel pick up your daddy's Mustang and bring it here. He bought that car years ago and gave me a spare key. He's always wanted Kalvin to have it once he gets out of the Marines. I'm not letting her keep that car. No way. No how. Marcel said that he will take me to visit your daddy whenever I want to go. If it's okay with you, can we use the Mustang? Marcel uses the bus to get to work and has no way to take me. I want to visit him today, poor thing."

"Yes, Granny. I'm sure Kalvin won't mind." That was the least of Layla's concerns. She was worried about her father and being on the east coast, so far away, made her feel helpless.

"Thank you, sweetie. I'll let you know how he is once I get to see him. I'll also have him call you."

"Do you know why he hasn't called me back? I've called several times." Layla was afraid of the answer.

"She took his phone away. She doesn't want anyone talking to him, especially me. She has no respect for anyone but herself. I told your father not to marry her, but he didn't listen."

The desperation in Granny Little's voice was surprising. She was the stalwart of the Little family; its long-time matriarch. Granny

Little rarely showed any signs of weakness. Since her youngest child passed away several years earlier, the strong, impenetrable person who was unshakable seemed to occasionally show signs of vulnerability that had never previously been displayed. Layla and the rest of the family were aware of it. Layla was now concerned that Granny Little feared the worst with her father. She wondered how his passing would impact her elderly grandmother.

"I'll talk to her. I promise, Granny."

◊ ◊ ◊

LAYLA DESPERATELY WANTED to visit her father in California but knew that she had to work. The nurses were contemplating striking. Layla had to cover for absent nurses should the union vote to strike. Now was not the time to be traveling. But that really wasn't the only reason why she needed to stay in New York. She also wanted to talk to the cardiologist that she worked with, Dr. Shapiro. He had taken a few days off from work for a mini vacation in the Hamptons. Once he came back to the hospital, Layla wanted to speak to him in person. In her mind, this would show Dr. Shapiro that she was serious about her father's treatment. Hopefully, Dr. Shapiro would give her father the priority position that she was requesting because he was in desperate need of a transplant. Going to Palmdale was certainly out of the question.

Despite that, Layla struggled with needing to talk to her father's latest wife in person. Maybe she could talk some sense into her. That was doubtful. Nevertheless, Layla needed to try to do something about Cissy's strange, impersonal response to her husband's needs. Layla vowed to her grandmother that she would speak to Cissy. Perhaps talking over the phone wasn't the best method to persuade Cissy to be compassionate and humane to her father, but it was the best that she could do at the moment.

Layla nervously fiddled with her phone until her fingers instinctively dialed her father's phone number. It rang and rang without being answered. Layla left a voicemail message:

"Cissy, this is Layla. David's oldest daughter. I'm here in New York and people are saying that my dad is doing really bad. He had a heart attack and needs a transplant. I need to know how he's doing. Can you call me? My number is 845-555-9166. Please call me."

Layla used her professional voice that was calming and reassuring. This was the voice that she mainly used at work, but rarely with her family and friends. She hoped that Cissy would be disarmed by her voicemail and would be considerate towards Layla's feelings. They never got along, but Layla rarely interacted with her father's women and never liked them. She was aloof with his many love interests. Living across the country didn't help. But it also shielded her from any conflicts. Now she could not avoid the conflict. Her father needed her, and she was the only one who could calmly explain why Cissy should step up as a wife. That was partly why her father got married in the first place.

Regrettably, Layla knew that she had to tell her children about the bad news about their grandfather. She would be meeting up with Amirah later that day for their weekly lunch and would tell her then. Kalvin was in Japan, fifteen hours ahead. So, she had to wait until it was appropriate to speak with him via FaceTime. Only Jasmine, her oldest needed to know right away. Layla called her immediately after pouring her morning coffee.

"Jazzy, its momma."

"Hey momma, it's good to hear from you. You called me early today. I wasn't expecting your call so soon." Jasmine looked towards her daughter, Cadence, to ensure that she was occupied and not getting into trouble. The rambunctious girl was four years old but bright and respectful.

"I know. I have some bad news about Papa Little."

In a calm voice, Layla explained the unfortunate news that her grandfather was gravely ill.

CONFLICT

MIDDLETOWN, NEW YORK

The Same Day

After getting off the phone with Jazmine, Layla noticed that she missed a text from Daniel. He was again telling her to enjoy her day and inquiring about her well-being. When she looked at the text, Layla was upset. She felt that Daniel was now becoming pushy. Daily texts used to be encouraging to her because it gave Layla a sense that Daniel desired her and longed to be with her. Now she felt like he was not respecting her privacy and not waiting until she responded to his message before texting again. She knew that Daniel lived alone. Perhaps his loneliness encouraged him to reach out to her when he should have been reaching out to family and friends.

"*I'm not his crutch,*" she thought with a hint of dismay.

A part of her regretted responding to his email. But subliminally, she reminded herself that Daniel wouldn't hurt her like other men that she dated or even married. That thought made Layla reevaluate her response. Maybe she was reacting too harshly to him and should instead simply respond with a terse message acknowledging his effort. And so, she did: "I'm ok."

"*There. That should keep him satisfied for the rest of the day.*"

When Layla received the "read receipt" notification and no response was forthcoming, she was quietly relieved. Now she could focus on more important things: Cissy.

Layla called her father's phone one more time. No answer. She texted her grandmother to get Cissy's personal cellphone number. Granny Little didn't have it. She then called her brother, Marcel, for the number. He didn't have it either. Who would? Layla thought long and hard for an answer. She was stumped for about an hour contacting various family members including in-laws. And then it came to her, "*Auntie Hilda should have the number.*"

Auntie Hilda was about the same age as Granny Little. She lived in Las Vegas. Layla's father and Cissy loved going to Las Vegas to gamble several times a year. They stayed with Auntie Hilda to save money. Auntie Hilda was not judgmental and embraced Cissy despite her many faults, which most of the other family members could not overlook. Layla knew that she had to contact Auntie Hilda. It was her last lead.

"Auntie, this is Lay." Layla addressed Hilda as her aunt even though she was really Granny Little's in-law.

"Child, it's good to hear your voice. How's my baby doing? You still in New York?"

Auntie Hilda always pressured Layla to move back to California to be closer to her family. But Layla loved her bi-coastal living; living in New York full time and spending the holidays in California. She could experience both cultures without sacrificing either. Besides, she had grown accustomed to the multiculturalism of New York that California was lacking in ways which she could not fully explain.

"Yes, Auntie. I'm loving the summer weather in New York."

"Ok, now. California has nice summers and better beaches."

"I know." Layla hesitated. She didn't want to continue this line of the conversation. "But I'm calling about my daddy. He's in a hospice. I've been trying to get a hold of Cissy."

"Oh, Lord. I hope he is okay."

"I don't know, Auntie. Cissy's not returning my calls. I need her number."

Auntie Hilda opened the top drawer to her end table and ruffled through tons of small pieces of white paper with scribbled numbers until she came to one that had "Rose Johnson" written on it.

"Here it is. I found it." She gave Layla Cissy's number.

"Thank you, Auntie."

"You're welcome. I'll be praying for your father. Let me know how he is doing. He was always my favorite."

"I will, Auntie. Love you."

Auntie Hilda rarely said that she loved anyone. It was something she stopped saying after her husband died years ago. They were just meaningless words to her. Actions showed love in her mind. "Ok, child. Have a good day."

After entering Cissy's number in her iPhone, Layla dialed it.

"Hello."

"Cissy, this is Layla."

"Layla?" Cissy's startled voice answered.

"I've left several messages for you, but you've never returned my calls."

"I've been busy."

"Busy doing what? Granny told me that you still haven't been to see David at the hospice. I'm very disappointed. He needs you."

"I didn't sign up for this. I'm not going to spend my nights at the hospice. I have to work and pay my bills. Are you going to pay my bills?"

"You don't work on the weekends and can visit him then at the very least. He's sacrificed everything for you, and he doesn't need this. He needs you now."

"There's nothing that I can do for him. I have my own issues that you don't know about. I don't need to give you an explanation."

Before Layla could finish saying: "Yes, you do. I am his daughter," Cissy ended the call. When Layla heard the phone become silent, she was livid. She wanted to call back and curse Cissy out but knew that she would not answer the phone. Layla assumed that Cissy already blocked her and probably everyone else in the Little family.

Frustrated and confused, Layla wondered what else she could do. She didn't expect a miracle from Cissy. At least Layla could tell Granny Little that she tried. That was all that could be expected.

Suddenly, Layla began to wonder about her own health and what would happen to her as she aged. Most of her children lived out of state or out of the country. Even Amirah, Layla's only child who still lived in New York, had plans to marry within the next few years. Amirah's boyfriend was from Michigan and he planned to raise a family there. Amirah visited a few times and loved it. She was not against moving away from New York for a better quality of life. Fortunately, she could transfer her job if she so desired. Layla realized that it was only a matter of time before she was alone in New York and could be in a worse position than her father. At least her father had elderly relatives who lived not too far from Palmdale.

A nagging feeling of uncertainty quietly consumed her. She had planned on being First Lady, but that wasn't likely. Her relationship with Roland was a farce all this time and now Daniel was a less than attractive option. Having a marriage was something that she wanted, but Layla was accustomed to being alone and being in charge of the family ever since her last divorce. It wasn't financial reasons that she wanted a partner. She wanted to be loved and to express her love.

CONFESSION

GILBERT, ARIZONA

The Next Week

Sleepy yet undeterred, Daniel drearily walked to his leather couch in the living room and lay down. He covered his entire body with a gray bamboo throw to keep him somewhat covered from the glow of the morning sun shining through the patio doors. He was a little under the weather but wanted to get out of the master bedroom with the hopes that, later in the day, he could do errands and finally clean the house. Unfortunately, his mind was occupied. He wondered why Layla wasn't answering his calls or returning his texts. When she did respond, her texts were curt, and she was unwilling to talk at any appreciable length. This was unlike her. So, Daniel was leery to reach out to her again. Instead, he tried to get some additional rest so that his body could recuperate.

"I should have made some *sancocho* last night," he thought regretfully. His mind could taste the root flavors of *yautia,* and yucca mixed with plantains and butternut squash. Although typically made with beef, Daniel cheated and used pork. It wasn't authentic to most Puerto Ricans, but Daniel preferred to use his favorite meat when cooking even when making traditional dishes. No one else could complain since they weren't eating it anyway.

Without any *sancocho* to eat, Daniel rose from the couch and put some water in his tea kettle to heat. He went into the pantry to bring out a flute of tupelo honey. The soft, buttery taste would sweeten the tea the way that Daniel enjoyed. What was missing were Valencian Magdalenas; the moist Spanish muffins with a hint of lemon would make a simple breakfast complete. Instead, Daniel had to be satisfied with a large mug of tea to warm his chilly body.

While waiting for the water to boil, he lay back down on the couch and closed his eyes. Before he could fall back asleep, his iPhone buzzed. Daniel wanted to ignore it. He turned the phone over without looking at the screen and then rolled over. In less than a minute, his phone buzzed again. Not wanting to seem like he was ignoring someone who wanted to talk (or needed legal advice), Daniel looked at his phone and saw the following text from Layla: "Can we talk?" He replied with: "Yes, call me whenever you want to talk."

His phone rang and Layla's familiar playful voice could be heard: "It's too long to type in a text so I wanted to talk to you over the phone. I hope you don't mind."

"No, I don't mind. How are you?"

Daniel resisted the urge to ask Layla why she hadn't returned his calls or most of his texts. He figured that she would give him an answer in due time. Something had to be on her mind if she was willing to call him. He wanted to find out what it was.

"I'm fine. Well, not really. It's been a hard few weeks."

This piqued his interest as well as intensified his concern for her.

"Oh, I'm sorry."

"Don't be sorry. It's not your fault, Daniel."

"I understand."

"My father is having some heart issues. Now only sixteen percent of his heart is pumping. He's had this issue for years. I've told him to go to the cardiologist, but he won't. He needs a transplant and I'm not sure if he will get one."

"Oh no. Why not?"

"Well, he hasn't done the work up to be on the transplant list. He was supposed to do it a while ago, but he put it off."

"I remember you mentioning this a year ago. Since you hadn't mentioned it again, I just assumed he was better. I'm sorry that he isn't better. I know you are close to your father."

"Thank you. He is my best friend. I talked to him again today. He is in bad shape. I told him that he should come to my hospital and have my doctor do the transplant."

"That's great. I'm sure he was happy that you made that offer."

"Well, Dr. Shapiro is willing to do it, but…" Layla's voice cracked as she spoke. "He's too weak to make the flight to New York. They told me that he wouldn't survive it."

She remained quiet for a moment. Daniel waited until she spoke again. He did not want to interfere with her obvious efforts to overcome opening up about her emotions and what she was dealing with these past few weeks.

"I… I… to be honest, … I'm glad that he won't be able to come."

"I don't understand."

Daniel could sense Layla's frustration as she was about to respond. But it was something other than frustration at the question itself but more a reluctance to admit her conflicting feelings; both shame and relief.

"I'm just so busy with work and my new manager position. I don't have time to take care of him. I work long hours and the commute is draining. It would be a full-time job taking care of my father once he gets the transplant."

"I see. There isn't anything wrong thinking about those things, Layla. Can he get the transplant in California?"

"If he was in New York, I could force him to do his work up for the transplant. But he won't go on his own. So, it doesn't look like he'll get the transplant after all if he stays in California."

"Why not?"

"I think he's scared and avoiding it makes him think it will go away and that he doesn't have an issue. But even if he does the work up, he doesn't have anyone to take care of him after the surgery."

"What about his wife? You said he was recently remarried."

"She's crazy and doesn't want to take care of him. Without a stable family life, he won't qualify for a transplant."

Daniel could hear Layla sniffling. He wanted desperately to hold her tight and comfort her. Being thousands of miles away was of no help. Even expressing his sorrow or dismay at the situation wasn't good enough. He was at a loss for words. Daniel understood that it was only a matter of time before Layla's father would succumb to his heart condition. Daniel was surprised that Papa Little had lived as long as he did, given his failing heart. It was a miracle of sorts that Layla had an extra two years to spend with her father. She expressed concerns that she had squandered the time; traveling to Puerto Rico with Daniel, worrying about Leon and Roland, and even visiting her granddaughter in Florida.

Despite these conflicting feelings, Daniel tried to reassure Layla that living life was okay, that she shouldn't feel guilty for not catering to her father, leaving her job and moving back to California to take care of him. Layla had a life to live too. She was entitled to live her life just like her father was entitled to live his life the way that he wanted to.

Whether the conversation made Layla feel better or not, Daniel did not know. Layla received a call from Granny Little and had to get off the phone.

THE HOSPICE

MIDDLETOWN, NEW YORK

Moments Later

When Layla switched from the call with Daniel to the other line with her Granny Little, she was apprehensive. Granny Little had previously told Layla that she was going to the hospice to visit her father that morning like she did every weekday. Layla was hoping that this call was going to be good news about her father. Typically, Granny Little stayed at the hospice until visiting hours were over. Marcel would pick her up and drive her home. When she arrived at her home in Long Beach, she would relax for a while. After eating a petite southern dinner, then she would call Layla for daily updates. By then, it was nearly midnight in New York. When Granny Little interrupted the call with Daniel, it was only noon in New York. It was unusual for Granny Little to call so early.

"Hey, Granny. How are you doing?" Layla said once it was clear that the first line had hung up and Daniel could not hear.

Layla tried to appear upbeat despite her doubts.

"I'm glad I could get a hold of you. I'm here at the hospice. It's not looking good for your father."

"Can you put the nurse on the phone? I want to speak to her."

"I wish I could. All of the nurses are in his room now. They asked me to leave."

"Where are you now?"

"I'm near the nurse's station."

"Is anyone there?"

"I don't think so. I think she went on a break. I haven't seen her in about five, no ten minutes."

Granny Little looked around in search of the station nurse. She saw an elderly man walking down the aisle with a little girl heading towards the rear of the hospice. The girl was almost gleefully skipping and laughing as she walked. The man struggled to catch up with her.

"Grandpa. Is she going to sing with me today?" The girl was no more than five years old, holding her grandfather's hand as she skipped towards the hospice room.

"Yes, Lilly. Grandma really wants to see you today. She misses you."

The girl smiled.

When the two were further away and their voices faded, Granny Little looked away so that she could locate the station nurse.

"Hold on, dear. I think she's coming back." Granny focused on a female figure heading towards her in the distance. "No, it's not her. It's a maintenance lady."

Upon hearing that disappointing revelation, Layla was perturbed with the lack of information. She refused to be angry at her elderly grandmother who had gone above and beyond at every turn. Now was not the time to make a fuss.

"Granny, can you call me back when you find out something? Anything?"

"Sure."

"I'm going to make some calls. I'll call you back right away. I promise."

"Thank you, Layla."

After ending the call, Layla tried to think of what she could do to learn about her father's status. She remembered speaking with the hospice director who had given Layla her direct line number after learning that Layla was a CTICU nurse. She dialed the number from her contact list but there was no answer. She also sent a text message to the director asking for an immediate callback. Before Layla could dial a second number, her iPhone rang. Layla answered.

"Layla, dear. He didn't make it. They couldn't revive him. I'm sorry but he's gone."

Granny Little began to cry profusely.

"Not another..."

The phone receiver dropped onto the floor making a loud thump that Layla could hear.

"GRANNY..."

When no response could be heard, Layla panicked. Moments later, Layla could hear the receiver scratching the flooring as it was grasped.

"Hello. Who am I speaking to?" A calm, female voice answered.

"This is Layla. Layla Little. My father, David Little, is a resident at the hospice. I was talking to my grandmother, Juanita Little. Is she okay?"

"Hold on."

Layla waited patiently for a response. She did everything she could to hold back her anger and frustration.

CEMETERY

MORENO VALLEY, CALIFORNIA

Two Weeks Later

"No, Auntie. I'm not sure if it's going to be an open casket." Layla's voice trembled when she spoke.

"Child. What are you talking about?" Aunt Hilda was confused by this comment. She assumed, like everyone else in the Little family, that they would be able to see David during the wake and personally say their goodbyes before he was interned at the Riverside National Cemetery.

"I know, Auntie. I don't understand myself. It's Cissy again. She's acting a fool."

"Oh, my goodness. What now?"

"She doesn't want to release the body to the family."

"Why not? Cissy doesn't want a funeral?"

"Yes. Well, yes and no. She wants her own funeral without the family there. She said that she's planning a small get together with her family."

"David didn't know her family. Why would they want to go to a funeral of someone they don't even know?" Aunt Hilda was progressively getting upset at this latest news. Nothing seemed to be going right after Papa Little died. The family was in a state of shock. Having to deal with Cissy's continued antics made things unbearable.

"I tried talking some sense into her. So far, it's not working."

"What are we gonna do? How are we going to have a funeral with no body? We can't have a funeral with an empty casket?"

Layla contemplated calling Cissy one more time to convince her. Perhaps this time it would work. But she wasn't too hopeful.

"Layla, David is a veteran. Can't the military help? He deserves to be buried with military honors. He would want that. We want that."

"I've told her that David will be buried in a military cemetery, but she's worried about the cost. She doesn't want to pay for it. She has no money."

"Please don't tell me that she wants to cremate him."

"I won't lie. She mentioned that but said that she hasn't made a decision yet."

Layla was being kind. She suspected that, if cost was truly an issue, then the only real option was cremation. Layla didn't know about Cissy's finances or whether she was just being cheap. Layla's father had life insurance which would easily cover the funeral expenses.

"I'm going to call the JAG. The military will pay for his entire funeral. There's no need to cremate David. She should know this. Money should not be an issue. How would your grandmother feel if she found out? It would break her heart"

Layla was secretly embarrassed. She knew that the military would pay for her father's funeral. He had mentioned it many times before. The added stress of dealing with Cissy and her own grief unexpectedly made Layla forget about this. Layla would not forgive herself if her father had to be cremated because she let her emotions cloud her judgment. She suspected that the family would not forgive her either, but she knew better. Her family was always loving and forgiving; at least to her.

◊ ◊ ◊

WHEN LAYLA OPENED the Facebook app on her iPhone, she scanned her newsfeed. Part of her wanted to post something about her father's passing. She had seen many posts of recent funerals for the many high school alumni who had passed away prematurely at an early age. The many conciliatory comments and sympathies engendered goodwill even in her own heart. But Layla could not bring herself to post anything about her father. It was a private affair that she felt she shouldn't be sharing online; at least not yet. Instead, she liked a few posts and then closed the app. She checked her text messages and nothing new was received except for the daily "hello" from Daniel. She chose to ignore it again because she did not want to talk to Daniel about her father.

Layla walked to the patio of her suite at the Ayres Hotel and Spa, which was overlooking the Moreno Valley Mall. She breathed in the crisp desert air as well as took in the views. Layla booked the boutique hotel because it was close to the Riverside National Cemetery; the only military cemetery for Southern Californian veterans. She originally wanted to be near her family in Long Beach but thought that it was better if she could host her family after the funeral should they need a place to emotionally unwind. No one complained about her choice.

But that decision left her alone and vulnerable. Layla's children couldn't come into town until the actual service was scheduled. Now, Layla had to plan the funeral service as best as she could with the continued uncertainty.

She had earlier ordered room service but lost her appetite after talking to Aunt Hilda. Hopefully, by the time the food was delivered, her appetite would return. But food was far from her mind. On her mind was writing the obituary, picking out a casket, arranging for flowers to be delivered, and determining who should be pallbearers. But Layla tried to suppress those thoughts. She wasn't in the mood to think about a funeral.

◊ ◊ ◊

It seemed like an hour passed but it was really only fifteen minutes. Tears welled up in her eyes. It was emotionally exhausting having to deal with her family, Cissy, and the funeral home. She was tired of hearing everyone's side or opinions. Layla just wanted it to all stop: the phone calls, the texts, posts on Facebook asking about her. She wished that she could forget it all. But she knew that even if she flew to the ends of the earth, she could not escape it. Her beloved father was still dead, and her grandmother was in the hospital from emotional exhaustion. They needed Layla to be strong now even if she did not want to be strong.

When it seemed as if she was finally making sense of it all, the unexpected happened. Her phone rang. No caller id appeared on her phone and the number was unfamiliar. She wondered who it was. Could it be another long-lost relative calling about her father? The hospital where Granny Little was admitted? Or Cissy? Trepidatious, she answered it not knowing who was calling.

"Hello."

"Lay, it's me."

"Leon?" Even in her exhausted state, Layla recognized his familiar voice.

"No, no. Don't hang up. Hear me out."

"What do you want?" Layla huffed. She was surprised at his call but intrigued, nonetheless.

"I heard about your father. I wanted to offer my condolences."

"Thank you, Leon." She didn't want to appear unappreciative.

"I was also calling because I wanted to offer my services for you and your family. I'm willing to do the funeral service free of charge."

Leon's chest appeared to have grown as he made the offer.

"What's the catch?"

"There's no catch." He hesitated but then continued in an effort to appear his usual confident self. "You mean a lot to me. I know that your father meant a lot to you. I just want to do something nice for you. You deserve it."

Layla wasn't sure if she believed Leon. He always had an ulterior motive when he did things for people. He wasn't always willing to admit his true reasons unless he absolutely had to. That was typically when he was cornered and had no alternative but to admit the truth.

"I don't know, Leon. I want this to be a happy occasion for me and my family. I'm going through a lot right now. I'm... I don't want to have to deal with any additional baggage."

"You mean me. Don't you?"

Leon was worried about the truth. But he had learned over the course of his therapy sessions that he had to accept someone else's truths and not just his own truth. He steadied himself for Layla's response.

"Leon, I don't really want to talk about it right now. I'll talk to my family about your offer, but to be honest, I think they already have someone in mind. But thank you again for your kind offer. I need to go."

"Ok, ok. Let me know what they decide."

"Sure."

Layla ended the call with additional, unnecessary angst. She regretted answering her phone.

VULNERABILITY

MIDDLETOWN, NEW YORK

Two Months Later

SEATED on Layla's front porch was Jeannie Thomas. She was sipping on some drink that she didn't know the name of and which she couldn't figure out what were the ingredients. It was a mixture of sweet and sour. Drinking it made her lips pucker because the taste was too strong and acidic. She wanted to throw it out but didn't want to offend her host.

"Layla, what is this?" Jeannie almost choked while speaking. "Layla!!" Jeannie spoke louder in hopes of getting Layla's attention. When no response was forthcoming, Jeannie turned her head towards the opened, front door; hoping to get a glimpse of her. Layla was nowhere to be found. So, Jeannie rose from her chair and walked into the house. "Layla. Layla. You there, sweetie?"

Jeannie scanned the living room looking for Layla. She walked further into the room and then into the kitchen.

"Layla." Jeannie's voice echoed.

A coffee pot was boiling, filling the kitchen with the bittersweet aroma of Arabica beans. Jeannie turned it off. She walked down the hallway towards the bedrooms in the rear of the house. The eerie silence was unbecoming, making her feel uncomfortable. She was unsure whether she was invading Layla's privacy. The knowledge that they were lifelong friends with very few secrets between them only encouraged Jeannie to walk further into the house. It was not as if a gentleman friend was with Layla. The two had been alone all day. No one had come for a visit.

Jeannie called out again as she reached the master bedroom. It was empty just like every other room that she had previously been in looking for Layla. Jeannie remembered that Layla had a basement with an office and a game room. She opened the basement door and walked down the wooden stairs. They creaked as she descended. When she reached the bottom of the stairs, Jeannie could see Layla lying on the ground in a fetal position, slightly rocking and clenching a picture in her hand.

Jeannie hurriedly ran toward Layla, turning her from her side onto her back. When their eyes met, Layla instantly snapped out of it. She recognized Jeannie.

"Hey, sweetie. You okay?"

"I don't know." Layla frantically wiped the tears from her cheeks and clumsily sat upright. "Thank you so much." She grabbed Jeannie's hand, squeezing it tightly. The picture dropped to the floor, revealing a smiling Layla alongside her smiling father.

Jeannie glanced towards the picture and picked it up.

"You guys look totally alike," Jeannie said as if it was something that she had not realized all these years.

Layla smiled. "All of the Littles have that same large forehead." Layla pointed to her forehead in the picture, encircling it with her finger to illustrate how big it was.

"It's more like a five- or a six-head." Jeannie couldn't keep herself from laughing. Layla also joined in the laughter.

"I really do miss him so much." Layla soft voice was barely discernible.

Jeannie leaned in to hug Layla. The tight hug allowed Layla to release her fears and hurts as if she was renewed in spirit.

"I know, sweetie."

Having lost her own father years earlier, Jeannie was very familiar with the whirlwind of feelings that Layla was struggling with. But like everyone else in the same position, Jeannie was at a loss for words. She tried desperately to remember what comforted her during her own trying time. But in all honesty, Jeannie remembered that nothing anyone said really brought comfort or alleviated the pain. Just having her friends and family with her was all that Jeannie needed after her father passed away. So, Jeannie did exactly that for Layla.

"Come upstairs. It's chilly down here." Jeannie stood up and motioned towards the stairs. She wanted to get Layla away from this area which must have triggered some internal turmoil. "I still want to know what's in that drink you gave me. It's nasty." A stupid expression effortlessly came upon Jeannie as she spoke.

"Oh my. My mistake. My mind was all over the place. I don't even remember what I put in it. I'm so sorry."

"No worries. I'll find something normal to drink."

Jeannie walked up the stairs and Layla instinctively followed.

"I'm a wreck and I know it." Layla leaned forward in her chair and stretched her arms towards the top railing on her porch. She turned her head towards Jeannie and stared intensely. "I don't know what to do."

"Don't be so hard on yourself. The funeral is over. Everything has been done already. What are you concerned about?"

Layla recounted to Jeannie the military funeral, how Cissy relented and allowed the family to bury his body at the Riverside National Cemetery, how the American flag draped over the cherry wood coffin, how the seven members of the honor guard each fired three volleys for a twenty-one gun salute, how a lone bugler played Taps solemnly, how the flag was presented to Granny Little after the coffin was lowered to the ground.

"It was a lovely service. He would be so proud." Layla sniffled but tried to hold it back. She was proud of herself for handling it all.

"Yes, it was. I'm so happy that it all worked out."

"I just don't know what to do with the rest of my life now that he is gone." Layla thought about her large empty home and her three adult children who had all moved away and moved on with their own lives.

Jeannie looked at Layla for a clue as to what was really on her mind. She waited without saying a word. When Layla realized that her friend knew something else was bothering her, she decided to finally discuss it.

"I'm going through a lot. I have my job. I just lost my dad, my best friend, but I keep getting texts and calls from Daniel. Even Leon calls me all the time."

Jeannie was surprised that Leon was still calling. Her ears perked up. A part of her knew that relationship talk was part of the reason Layla invited her to New York again, even if Layla didn't originally come out and say why she wanted Jeannie to visit.

"These men think that I'm thinking about marriage or being in a relationship right now. I'm not. That's the last thing on my mind."

"I totally know what you mean. Are they at least understanding about how you feel and what you are going through?"

"I haven't been returning Daniel's calls or texts. So, I don't know what he's thinking. I'm hoping that he will just give up after a while."

"He does like you a lot, Layla. He's waited a long time to be with you. But Daniel seems like the kind of guy who will respect your wishes. He'll figure it out and leave you alone; if that's what you want." Jeannie brought a glass to her mouth to sip but looked intently over the top of the glass towards Layla as she drank so she could see Layla's reaction to the last comment.

Layla was stoic and unfazed. That surprised Jeannie.

"Daniel will get over it. I don't think Leon will. We have a connection that I don't fully understand. He gets me, Jeannie, like no one else does. I can't describe it. He knows what I'm thinking before I say it. We have the same passion and desire for the ministry. He makes me laugh and laughs at my jokes. He knows that I want to be married again. I'm not sure if Daniel does. He hasn't talked about it with me yet even though I have hinted about wanting to get married someday."

Jeannie listened attentively. She refused to let her face react to Layla's statements and reveal her personal concerns. She wanted Layla to feel comfortable sharing.

"Sounds like you've been accepting Leon's calls."

"Yes, I have. I told him that I'm not ready. He understands."

"That's good. Just relax and have fun. Be in touch with yourself again and what you want in life. You don't have to rush into anything. It's okay to wait. And whatever is meant to work out, will. If not, then it wasn't meant to be."

"You're right. I don't want to be pressured into anything. And I especially don't want to make another mistake. I'm going to do me. Nothing wrong with that."

Jeannie agreed.

The two ladies talked about whether to go into the city that night. They decided against it and agreed to stay at home enjoying each other's company.

REFLECTION

GILBERT, ARIZONA

Several Months Later

"Praise Him!"
"Praise Him, everyone; Young and Old."
"Praise Him! "
"Praise Him, everyone; With Voices Untold."
"Praise Him in the morning."
"Praise Him in the evening."
"Praise Him all night and all day."

THE SMALL CHOIR jubilantly sang a new hymnal recently penned by their own Pastor Leon Blackman. The tambourines' jingling rattles could be heard even over the shouts of church members and attendees who were standing and singing along. Some were wailing as they were struck by the Holy Spirit. Others were swaying to the music with both arms lifted up towards heaven as if to signify their heartfelt praise.

The congregation in attendance was anywhere from thirty to fifty souls, all worshipping together. Standing in the front row was Layla. Her long flowing, black church dress covered her legs almost to her ankles. Her black Gucci handbag was laid on the pew. Seated next to her was Willie May Jefferson, an older woman who became Layla's close friend when she first started dating Leon nearly eight years ago. Willie May was happy to see Layla again. They talked occasionally after Layla broke off the relationship when Leon did not want to get engaged or publicly acknowledge the relationship. But it had been years since Willie May actually saw Layla since the night of the graduation party celebrating his doctorate.

Admittedly, Willie May was surprised to see Layla sitting in her old position in the front pew where the First Lady would normally sit. It gave her mixed feelings. Why was Layla back in Leon's life? Was she here to stay? Were they going to finally get married? Was Layla going to move back to Arizona? Whatever was going to happen in the future, although a friend to Layla, Willie May wanted, most of all, to see her pastor happy. But she didn't want to see him hurt again, the way he seemed secretly devastated when the relationship ended.

After the breakup, Layla's absence was obvious to any regular church attendee. Pastor Blackman didn't formally address it with the congregation. Instead, he told a few church members whom he was closer to; mainly the males that he discipled and, of course, Dr. Johnson, his mentor. But like all small churches, the gossip spread like wildfire. Everyone eventually learned of the breakup but not the reason why. No one dared inquired why the relationship ended.

After the Sunday service was over, Leon approached Layla with his typical beaming smile. "They loved me. I know that I touched a lot of people today. I could see it in their spirit."

"It was a great sermon, Leon." Layla reached out to touch Leon's shoulder, but before she could, he instinctively moved towards Willie May without acknowledging Layla's affection.

"Wonderful! Wonderful, Pastor!" Willie May exclaimed with a southern charm that easily betrayed her Creole background.

"Thank you, Sister Jefferson." Leon gave the elderly woman a hug and then reached out to the person seated next to her. It was his habit to greet every attendee before they exited the church. Sometimes it would take upwards of an hour to do so if the church was at full capacity. Today, it was not. The attendees who frequented the church on occasion eventually learned to sit in the back of the church so that they could quickly sneak out without anyone noticing and avoid the tradition. Most wanted to leave ahead of the Sunday lunch crowd. Some just wanted to avoid being touched for fear of germs. Others wanted to get home as quickly as they could so that they could see the game. But a majority of the church attendees enjoyed this unique tradition because it gave them a chance to personally interact with Pastor Blackman and feel connected to the church. They stayed as long as it took to say farewell to the pastor.

Layla had forgotten about this ritual. She stood patiently watching Leon hug or shake hands with everyone, one pew at a time. Often, the men would put an arm around their pastor and smile. Their wives would give a polite church hug, not too tight and not too close. The widow, Maya Smith, who had danced with Leon at his graduation party, seemed to hug Leon tighter and closer than Layla remembered her doing on previous occasions. That perturbed Layla but she tried not to visibly show it.

In the far back row, on the left side of the church, stood Marlo. She was glaring intensely at Layla and huffing underneath her breath. Layla didn't see Marlo while she was watching Leon because Marlo was outside of her peripheral vision. *I can't believe she is here. I'm so mad.* Marlo's teeth clenched as the thought clouded her mind and filled her with rage. Given their recent conversations, she had believed that Leon had finally gotten over Layla. Marlo was apparently mistaken and knew nothing of their recent rekindled relationship.

"Are you okay?" An elderly man said after he noticed Marlo's legs and arms nervously shaking.

"Leave me alone, you... you ole granddad," she quipped.

"That's not very Christian-like," he retorted.

Marlo marched out of the church, almost pushing the gentleman as she left. She then drove home.

◊ ◊ ◊

WHILE LAYLA DROVE her rental car from the church to Downtown Gilbert, Leon sat on the front passenger's seat. He typically allowed her to drive because it subconsciously made him feel chauffeured, but he never told that to Layla. Instead, he let her feel as if she was in control.

As they were driving up Gilbert Road, he turned to her saying, "I'm glad that we can finally get some good Mexican food. This place is great."

"I've never been to Barrio Queen. I think it was a great idea." Layla's lips hinted at a smile. She kept looking forward as she drove.

"Yes, it is. The tacos are the best. They have homemade corn tortillas. And the guacamole? Man, it's good. Best I ever had. They make it fresh right at the table."

The way Leon's eyes gleamed as he talked about the guacamole made Layla suspicious. Leon had never taken her to this restaurant before, but he was very familiar with it. Sure, it had been more than four years since they last dated. Leon had plenty of opportunities to go to Barrio Queen with his visiting pastors, male disciples, or with his brother, Joseph. But the way that he excitedly spoke of this partic-ular restaurant made Layla suspect that Leon had taken a woman for dinner there and had fond memories of the encounter. He rarely splurged by going to nicer restaurants unless it involved a woman. Certainly, not for his brother.

Layla's suspicions only heightened her underlying feelings of mistrust that she tried to suppress. But she couldn't hold the fact that Leon had seen other women against him when they hadn't been dating each other. She had dated Roland and Daniel during that same timeframe. Layla knew that Leon was willing to overlook her past relationships and that she should overlook his past relationships as well. However, Leon had cheated on her several times during their relationship. Or at least, she had suspected that he had. That difference made rekindling their relationship more difficult. Layla honestly knew that she had internal struggles to overcome, not to mention the emotional issues involving the physical abuse that she endured at Leon's hand. Had she truly forgiven him? Could she ever forgive him? Should she forgive him? Layla knew that he was going to counseling for his anger management. He seemed different. But was it genuine? Was it enough? Was it too late?

She wanted to forget those thoughts and just enjoy the evening with him.

DANIEL CHECKED his Facebook newsfeed and noticed that Layla had earlier checked into the First Conservative Baptist Church of the Valley. His facial expression clearly exhibited disappointment mixed with regret.

RESOLUTE

GILBERT, ARIZONA

The Same Day

AFTER A FILLING TRADITIONAL MEXICAN MEAL, they headed back to Leon's home in Mesa. Layla was suspiciously quiet during the ride home. She had noticed that Leon checked his cellphone several times during the meal and that he was distracted. He even wanted to dismiss himself from the table, but Layla insisted that he stay with her and that he focus his attention on her rather than others. She explained that she deserved it. She flew the four-hour, red-eye flight from New York to spend the weekend with him at her own expense. She had always flown to visit him at her own expense. Leon never offered to pay for any of the flights or the rental cars. Perhaps, he justified it because Layla, as an assistant nurse manager at a big city hospital, made four to five times more money than he did. Even knowing this, it still caused Layla some underlying resentment. At the very least, Leon could simply offer to pay even if he could not afford to pay. He did not. Layla would, of course, politely decline. But it would have made her feel better knowing that she was with a man who would provide financially even if it wasn't all the time.

After dating Daniel, who regularly paid for their outings: dinners, movies, live theater, gifts; and who would eagerly pay to fly to New York to visit her, Layla now had a different view of courtship. That inevitably soured her towards Leon. But she realized that it wasn't fair to Leon if she did not let him know. He wasn't a mind reader and couldn't guess what she was thinking or feeling. Layla had hoped that his counseling sessions would give Leon a greater insight into how relationships work and encourage him to ask her about her feelings or evaluate his actions. Apparently, that hadn't changed. At least not yet.

As they arrived at his house and exited the car, Layla noticed that Leon did not open her car door or even close it for her. He headed straight to his front door excited for some other reason. He was at his front door before Layla was able to grab her Gucci bag, close and lock the driver-side door, and put her keys away. When she looked around to see where Leon was, she could barely see his left shoe before the screen door closed behind him. She followed him inside and closed the hardwood, front door.

"Leon," she said as she laid her Gucci bag on the coffee table, looking for him.

"I'm in the bedroom, getting this suit and tie off." His voice could be heard coming from the back of the house as well as the thump of shoes hitting the floor when he kicked them off. "Help yourself if you need anything. Are you going to change into something comfortable?"

Layla was unsure. Before she could respond, she saw Leon's phone lying on the coffee table as well. He had apparently not taken his phone with him to his master bedroom like he normally did.

"*I shouldn't look at his phone,*" she thought as soon as she saw it. "*I might not be prepared for what is on it. What if...*" Layla remembered chatting with Jeannie about this. "If you suspect your man of cheating, he probably is," Jeannie would tell her. It was women's intuition. Every woman knew that.

Layla grabbed Leon's phone. Her heart palpitated immensely. She had never dared look at his phone before even though she had many opportunities to check its contents when Leon wasn't around. But some gnawing feeling encouraged her to check the phone this time. *"Who was he texting during lunch?"* She needed an answer.

The phone was locked. When the passcode was required, Layla was initially stumped. She first entered Leon's mother's name as the passcode, but it didn't work.

"How could I be so stupid?" She remembered that Leon's relationship with his mother was strained. They had not talked about it for years, but Layla realized that perhaps things had still not changed. For a moment, Layla was about to enter her own name as the passcode. She knew Leon was bad at remembering numbers and that the passcode had to be the name of someone that he cared deeply about and whose name he could easily remember. But afraid that she might accidentally lock out the phone, Layla decided against it. She then entered "S-O-P-H-I-A." When the phone unlocked, she was surprised and relieved at the same time.

Sophia was Leon's oldest granddaughter. "My heart" as he often referred to her with a glowing smile to anyone who listened, especially the single, female members at his church. Layla was glad that the passcode wasn't another woman's name.

She nervously opened the messaging app and anxiously checked the top entry. The name was "Okevia Peterson." Layla thought hard and fast for the names of the female church members, but that name was unfamiliar to her. She thought that the top name would be the young widow, Maya Smith. Fortunately, it wasn't.

Layla could hear more rumbling coming this time from the master bathroom. Leon was apparently preoccupied with relieving himself. He often read the Bible or a church magazine when he was on the porcelain throne. This meant Layla had more time to investigate. She took advantage of that extra time.

She opened the conversation with Okevia and read the text message exchange:

OKEVIA: How's my baby doing today? Sorry, I couldn't make church today. I'll be there next weekend like I always am.

LEON: No worries, my love. I'm entertaining a visiting pastor from New York. Don't have much free time this weekend. Can't wait to see you next weekend.

OKEVIA: Hope your sermon went well today.

LEON: Yes, it did. They let loved me.

OKEVIA: I'm so proud of you!! Can't wait to be your First Lady.

LEON: It's only a matter of time.

OKEVIA: Love you ???

LEON: Love you too 🖤

"*FIRST LADY!!*" Layla was livid. When Leon encouraged Layla to have faith in him and renew their relationship, he also promised her that she would be his only one and that, in time, he would publicly acknowledge their relationship and make her his First Lady. He obviously had no intention of doing that. Layla finally realized that now.

She stormed into the master bedroom and knocked on the bathroom door. Water could be heard splashing against the sink and then the sound of a towel being wiped. Leon opened the door with his typical, grinning smile.

"Ah, now I'm refreshed." He was now dressed in jeans and a T-shirt. He paused as soon as he noticed that Layla's brown eyes were bulging and her nostrils flaring.

"Oh, so who's Okevia?" Layla angrily questioned Leon in a voice atypical of her gentle demeanor.

"I... I... It's no one." Leon stuttered.

Layla firmly pressed his cellphone onto Leon's chest, saying "Don't lie to me. I read the texts already."

Leon slumped as he walked to his bed and sat down.

"I was going to tell you about her. I haven't broken it off yet because she is in a fragile state. She's going through a lot right now." Leon was hoping to explain Okevia's struggles and his concerns that he did not want to add to the situation at this time.

"A fragile state? I'm in a fragile state. I just lost my dad a few months ago. I told you that Leon. You said that you understood. You don't."

"I'll dump her. I promise. I'll do it now. Do you want me to call her?" He frantically looked for his cellphone which was on the ground so that he could place the call.

"Leon, it's too late. You keep doing this to me. I don't know why I keep falling for your lies. Jeannie was right."

At the sound of Jeannie's name, Leon almost lost it. He remembered accusing Layla of being a lesbian when Jeannie visited her in New York last year. At the time, his unchecked jealousy and insecurities made him think such inappropriate things. He tried not to let his brewing anger control him anymore. He needed to be in control of his own thoughts and actions and subdue them before speaking. But it wasn't enough. The contortions on his face while thinking of Jeannie scared Layla. They brought up fears of his past abuse.

"I'm going," Layla said anxiously.

She walked so fast to her rental car that the screen door slammed hard behind her. Leon watched mesmerized as she speedily drove away.

◊ ◊ ◊

AFTER THE "SEAT BELT" light turned off once the plane leveled off at around thirty-thousand feet, Layla reclined her seat the few inches it was allowed to. She was pleasantly surprised that the airline had an early flight back to New York. The reservation change fee was steep but worth it. Layla didn't feel like staying in Arizona one minute longer after learning of Leon's betrayal. She drove straight to Sky Harbor Airport after leaving Leon's house. He had not called her before the flight took off. Now that she was in the air, he could not disturb her during the four-hour flight across the country.

Layla closed her eyes, trying to sleep but it was difficult, not just because of the small, uncomfortable seats, but also because her mind wandered. She kept envisioning Leon and all the pain that she endured, making her restless.

She opened her eyes and looked around the cabin. Most people were relaxing, listening to music, or watching a movie on their phone. Some were sleeping like a baby despite the heavy rattling and sudden shakes of the plane. Layla looked into the seat pocket in front of her for something to read. She glanced at the safety card but had read the card many times over her numerous travels. She moved the airsickness bag and pulled an American Way magazine out. Flipping through the pages, she unexpectedly stopped at an article about San Juan, Puerto Rico.

Photos of *El Morro* and the Bacardi Rum Factory reminded her of her recent trip. She remembered Daniel and her walking along the cobblestone streets of San Juan. She remembered the boat ride to *Palominitos* Island and the smell of the salty, Caribbean waters. But most of all, she remembered relaxing on the beach by herself when the blue butterfly, majestic and serene, landed on her right hand. Its imprint was still on her mind filling her with hope now, reminding her of new beginnings, new dreams to unfurl.

She was resolute. No more Leon. No more dating, at least for a while. No more pain and sorrow. Just the future to face; an unending set of tomorrows where she could begin again, love again, try anew again, see clearly again, learn to be free again. She promised herself hope. She promised herself that she needed professional help. She needed someone who could talk her through the pain, talk her through forgiveness, even forgiveness for herself so that she could say goodbye to the past, at least the painful parts of it. Someone who could help her mourn the loss of her father and the loss of her innocence.

SAN DIEGO

SAN DIEGO, CALIFORNIA

One Year Later

EARLIER, Layla had a continental breakfast *al fresco* by herself in a cafe overlooking La Jolla Shores. After seeing the spectacular views from her table, she decided that she would change her plans from shopping to walking along the beach. Feeling the crisp, ocean water between her toes when she tested the waters, Layla realized that it was a smart decision.

The waves crashed mightily onto the beach. As she walked casually with no real sense of purpose on the soft sand, Layla could see cliffs far in the distance just north of La Jolla Cove. A dozen or so seagulls flew in unison. Layla watched as the seagulls landed on the beach scavenging for insects and crustaceans that rose to the surface when the crashing waves surrendered themselves back into the Pacific Ocean. The smell of salt filled her nostrils every time she took a breath. It was refreshing.

Over the roaring sounds of the waves, Layla could still hear her heart beating, giving her a sense of awareness, not only of her bodily rhythms but also of her inner mental thoughts. She wanted to walk along the beach to relax and escape it all. The past year for her was too stressful but her reward after long hours of self-reflection and strenuous work was a mini vacation on the west coast. Today was her last full day in San Diego. She would fly back to New York in the morning and would then have to face reality again. But for now, she could simply enjoy the scenery and the fresh air.

Although normally crowded, La Jolla Shores was nearly empty this time of year. Only a few strangers walked the beach or played in its waters. She welcomed the alone time but wished for more. Gone were the doubts that love was unattainable. Gone were the feelings that somehow, she did not deserve love, true love. Gone were the aches and pains from past loves that neglected her and focused instead on their own devices.

Layla was whole again, happy again, filled with passion and the zest for life like she had from years past. She was revitalized. Her counselor saw it. Her friends and family and even her co-workers saw the new Layla. They liked that about her.

But despite that, she felt guilty for wanting to be loved once more. Being independent was what she was told she needed to be. A man was more of an accessory, not a necessity. To a certain extent, she agreed.

As she walked closer towards the Scripps Pier, Layla noticed a few kayakers launching from the beach. She watched as they paddled out to sea. It reminded her of Puerto Rico and the kayaking trip that she enjoyed. Looking closer, Layla suddenly realized that there was a familiar figure on the horizon.

"*It couldn't be,*" she thought intensely.

Layla focused on one particular person who was laughing and encouraging the kayakers on from the shore. His smile was reminiscent of a smile that she had seen the previous year, but she was not sure given the orientation of his body away from her and towards the kayakers. Her pace quickened along with the quickening of her heartbeat. When she was less than ten feet from the mysterious person, he suddenly turned towards her when he heard footsteps. His eyes lit up upon recognizing her.

"Layla! What are you doing here? It's good to see you."

She walked closer. Her head tilted down with a slight smile. She tossed her hair to the side to see him better.

"Hi, Daniel. I'm surprised to see you too. I was just here for the weekend. It's funny that you're here too."

Daniel explained that he was visiting some old college buddies who were now attending the Scripps Institution of Oceanography nearby. He wanted to see them one more time before his caseload at work picked up and he no longer had the opportunity to take time off to relax.

"Why didn't you go kayaking?" Layla asked. "You were good at it in..."

"... Puerto Rico," Daniel added. His smile brightened even more. "Yeah, I haven't been kayaking since." Daniel looked off into the distance as if he was avoiding eye contact with Layla. She noticed his sudden uneasiness.

Daniel turned back to Layla and with a gentle voice said, "I've missed you, Layla. You've always been special to me even after all these years."

Layla stood next to Daniel and grabbed his hand, holding it tight.

"I'm completely flattered," Layla said as she gazed deeper into his eyes. "We've had our bumps in the road."

"I understand that. I just hope that you've understood my strong feelings for you over the years." Daniel was unsure of Layla's feelings for him at that moment. But he had vowed to himself that he would tell her how he felt the next time that they met. He could not back down now. She needed to know how he felt about her even if it meant that she would reject him again. "I know it sounds like I'm desperate for your love and affection. I apologize for that."

"No, it doesn't. I wish that I hadn't wasted so much precious time with men who didn't deserve me." Layla now had a sheepish look on her face.

"To be honest, you're a rare woman and no one really deserves someone as precious as you. Even myself."

"Don't make me cry," Layla sniffled as she spoke.

"If you do cry, I will kiss away your tears."

Daniel wrapped his left arm around Layla's waist and held her tightly for a long time. He then turned her body towards him, embraced her, and kissed her; a deep longing kiss as if it was their first time.

Layla shivered as they kissed. They continued to embrace until Daniel opened his arms letting her body go. He held her hand and led her towards the pier. They continued walking side by side, laughing and catching up over what they missed in each other's lives the previous year.

THE END

Dear reader,

We hope you enjoyed reading *Butterflies Blue*. Please take a moment to leave a review, even if it's a short one. Your opinion is important to us.

Discover more books by Daniel Maldonado at https://www.nextchapter.pub/authors/daniel-maldonado

Want to know when one of our books is free or discounted for Kindle? Join the newsletter at http://eepurl.com/bqqB3H

Best regards,

Daniel Maldonado and the Next Chapter Team

You might also like:
The Global View by W.L. Liberman

To read the first chapter for free, head to:
https://www.nextchapter.pub/books/the-global-view-literary-fiction

ABOUT THE AUTHOR

Mr. Maldonado is an attorney in the Phoenix area that has practiced insurance coverage and employment discrimination law. He is a co-author/editor of Couch on Insurance, a multi-volume treatise on insurance law. Mr. Maldonado is also a contributing author on CAT Claims: Insurance Coverage for Natural and Man-Made Disasters. Mr. Maldonado also wrote the employment chapter for the Arizona Tort Law Handbook. He has contributed to various law reviews and other articles. Now, Mr. Maldonado takes his hand to an area of personal satisfaction: relationships and emotional experiences.

Check out his Author Page:
https://danielmaldonadoauthor.wordpress.com

Check out his Amazon Author Central page:
https://www.amazon.com/Daniel-Maldonado/e/B004XW3DDM/

Like and Follow him on Facebook:
https://www.facebook.com/DanielMaldonadoAuthorPage/

Follow him on Twitter:
https://twitter.com/DanielMalAuthor

Follow him on Goodreads:
https://www.goodreads.com/author/show/14367577.Daniel_Maldonado

Follow him on Instagram:
https://www.instagram.com/danielmaldonadoauthor/

Follow him on SoundCloud:
https://soundcloud.com/daniel-maldonado-author

BIBLIOGRAPHY

This is a list of books and short stories written and published by Daniel Maldonado:

The Palace of Winds and Other Short Stories - A collection of poignant short stories addressing romance, failures, intrigues, and beliefs from a male perspective. My Book

Through Thunder and Light - A follow up to the original compilation "The Palace of Winds and Other Short Stories." My Book

From the Streets of Chambers Lane - The intriguing story of the Mendoza family's unexpected loss of their youngest son and sibling, Michael. Dealing with spiritual struggles and disillusionment as well as familial rivalries and quirky social interactions, the novella introduces the reader to each diverse family member's perspective of the tragic event while personalizing their cultural past and fears of the unknown future. http://mybook.to/ChambersLane

When Dreams Abound: A Return to Chambers Lane - Fatherless, Daniel Mendoza learns from a myriad of male friends and neighbors who come into his life from childhood to adulthood about what it actually means to be a man. http://mybook.to/DreamsAbound

The Prodigal Son From Chambers Lane - The oldest son, Jose Luis Mendoza, Junior, battles a haunting past secret that has hindered his growth even into his adult years. He must confront his unloving and hard-hearted mother and others who have betrayed his desire to be loved before he is able to escape it and embrace his future. http://mybook.to/ProdigalSon

Butterflies Blue: An Interlude in San Juan, Puerto Rico - While vacationing on the tropical Caribbean island of Puerto Rico with her newest boyfriend,

Layla unexpectedly encounters her former jealous boyfriend, Leon, who desperately wants her back

Dear reader,

Thank you for spending your time reading *Butterflies Blue: An Interlude in San Juan, Puerto Rico.* I value your word of mouth and appreciate any efforts you can expend to let others know about my books. If you enjoyed this book, please consider supporting me by doing any of the following:

Please leave a book review on Amazon.com (also for your country's version of Amazon if different), Goodreads, BookBub, and any other book site that you use to help market and promote this book;

Please tell your family, friends, co-workers, and colleagues about this author and his books;

Please share brief posts on your social media platforms and tag the book (#ChambersLane) and/or the author (#DanielMalAuthor) on Twitter, Facebook, Instagram, WordPress, etc.

Please suggest the book for book clubs, book stores, schools, or to any local libraries that you know.

Again, thank you in advance for your support. I look forward to reading your review and hope you enjoy the rest of the series and my other books.

9 781715 058302